COLOR HIM GUILTY

Color Him Guilty

Joe L. Hensley

Walker and Company
New York

Copyright © 1987 by Joe L. Hensley

All rights reserved. No part of this book may be reproduced or transmitted in any form or by any means, electronic or mechanical, including photocopying, recording, or by any information storage and retrieval system, without permission in writing from the Publisher.

All the characters and events portrayed in this story are fictitious.

First published in the United States of America in 1987 by the Walker Publishing Company, Inc.

Published simultaneously in Canada by John Wiley & Sons Canada, Limited, Rexdale, Ontario.

Printed in the United States of America

Library of Congress Cataloging-in-Publication Data

Hensley, Joe L., 1926–
   Color him guilty.

   I. Title.

PS3558.E55C6   1987   813'.54   86–24657
ISBN 0–8027–5670–0

10 9 8 7 6 5 4 3 2 1

Author's Note

More years ago than I like to admit, I wrote and sold a book called *The Color of Hate*. It appeared on the racks in paperback for a few weeks in 1960 and did fairly well, as such things go. It was a book about a northern lawyer just moved to a small southern town and appointed to defend a black man accused of a brutal rape and murder. It was also my first book.

A year or so back, I decided the world had changed enough for me to change that novel. I wanted to retell the story in the perspective of today. While it's the *same* story, its events are viewed in a very different light by its characters, by me; and will also be, I'm sure, by its readers. So I poured it into my Kaypro Ten and began to revise.

In the years since I wrote that first book, I've done a lot of different things. I've served one term in the Indiana General Assembly, and was a prosecutor for four years. In 1977 I became a circuit judge (and am still one). I may not be a better writer than I was in the late fifties, but I know more about how the law works and how people react to it. I've also written and sold a dozen other suspense novels. Some have been reprinted in paperback, some as foreign or book-club editions. And yet that first book kept coming back to me.

What I suppose I'm trying to say is that I liked that first book, but I thought I could do it better a second time around. Putting it on the computer didn't make it easy, but it made it easier.

So here it is. I like it better now and my soul is content. And some nice people at Walker liked it also and thought it was worthy enough to take on.

I hope that whether you saw that first one or not (and the chances of that are remote), you'll like this version.

—Joe L. Hensley
Madison, Indiana
1986

1

It was one of those misty southern mornings. I got to the office at about nine o'clock, after walking the three blocks from my rented apartment. The sign on the door was bright and shiny, and it read in gold leaf: Samuel April, Atty. It had cost fifty bucks. I'd just had it put on a few months before. For another ten the painter had offered to add "At Law," but I didn't think that was necessary. In a town of seventeen thousand, everyone knows who you are and what you do even if you've only been with them a year or so.

I kicked my feet up on the battered desk and dug through the mail I'd not opened for several days. There was a stern letter from the state bar association telling me my dues were delinquent, three advertisements for legal books, and a note from the local historical society asking me to attend a gala and pay twenty-five bucks therefor. I deposited them all where they'd do the most good.

There weren't any checks, but then there seldom were. My business consisted largely of women seeking divorces, who, for one reason or another, were angry at the other lawyers in town. And of course there were collections cases, many of which I received, few of which I collected. . . .

But was I discouraged?

That's right; I was.

At nine-thirty I observed ritual. I closed and locked the office and went out for coffee. Usually I meet Doc

Mahoney at that time. I put an optimistic sign up on the door that says I'll be back by ten o'clock.

The sun had come out in the time I'd spent in the office and I immediately felt better. I've got some holes in my chest where a Cong machine-gunner hemstitched me because I was in the wrong place at the wrong time. Mahoney, my M.D. friend, who's also a bachelor—which may explain why we're friends—says that if the small-caliber slugs had been a few inches lower, wet weather wouldn't bother me. Nothing, in fact, would bother me. But now, when it was wet, the scars ached. So I looked up at the sun and said hello.

I like a small town. I like knowing many of the people in it—the good ones and the bad ones—even if they don't come to me for advice. I walked the short distance to the coffee shop and saw some I knew, and we nodded and smiled at each other. I consoled myself with the idea that if I never got rich in this town, still I'd never work myself to death.

At this time of morning the coffee break was the accepted thing and Mac's was the accepted place. At election time we argued politics; every summer it was the Braves and how they'd do. There was time for football, nuclear missiles, the latest death—and always the latest dirty story.

Mahoney was already there, but he was with a bunch of people in the back. I stood for a moment, but when he failed to see me, I sat down by myself. I knew almost immediately something was wrong. I could feel it.

Mac came up.

"One with cream, Mac."

He leaned toward me. "They doing anything about it over there yet?"

I raised my eyebrows. "Doing anything about what?"

"About that black bastard that raped and killed the Cunnel girl Saturday night. Ain't you heard?"

I'd never seen Mac angry before. He's one of those placid types who seldom raise their voices. And I'd never heard him bad-mouth minorities before either, although I'd listened to a joke or two in that vein from him. I stared up at him. "I haven't been to the courthouse this morning, and I was out of town over the weekend. So no, I haven't heard anything about it."

"The local cops found her down by the graveyard early Sunday morning. She'd been raped and then axed to death. They've got Little Al Jones over in jail. The cops caught him. He lives real close to where it happened." He shifted the spatula to his other ham hand. "Some of the crowd in here is pretty upset about it. They've been talking about what needs to be done. Daughters ain't safe on the streets no more."

I stared at him. "If that means what I think it means, then 'some of the boys' better button their fat lips. Those days are gone."

He looked me over like he was maybe seeing me for the first time, but he didn't say anything else. He brought my coffee silently and went back to talk to the group of customers who were sitting, angry-faced, at the other end of the counter. Doc Mahoney was one of them, but his face was expressionless. The others were asking questions, and Doc was carefully answering them. Finally I got his eye and he picked up his cup and came on up.

"Good morning, Coroner," I said.

He smiled, revealing fine teeth. He's a very handsome man, a little older than I am. He could, when he wanted to be charming, be the best in the world and we'd had a lot of fine times together. His main fault was that he seldom saw anyone else in his mirror. All intelligence was graded in comparison to his own, and therefore failing. Yet he hid it well and he had quite a following. I liked him.

"Some excitement over the weekend," he said softly. He nodded toward the other end of the counter. "The savages are restless, but then savages usually are."

"You check it? The body, I mean?"

"Yeah." He smiled and rubbed hands over tired eyes. "All legal-like. Long hours. Where you been you didn't hear all about it?"

"I drove into the city."

He smirked. "And I guess the radio in your Chevy is still out." He looked down at his watch. "Got to get to the hospital." He downed the rest of his coffee and got up. "See you at the City Club for lunch?"

I nodded and drank my coffee morosely. I'd known the Cunnel girl slightly. I'd even been at a party or two where she'd been present. Not bad. The eyes were especially good; soft and vulnerable and seeking. She'd been a secretary for a time in Sanders's office. Sanders had been the oldest member of the local bar when I'd first come to town and had died while I was still seeking office space. Julia Cunnel had even come in to see me some weeks afterward about a job. I'd been flattered that she thought I could afford a secretary. Her answers to my questions had been warm, perhaps too warm. Now she was dead and I was sorry she was dead. But I was sorrier for the people in the back of Mac's place with their old-time ideas.

Little Al Jones I'd never heard of.

They were getting loud again at the other end of the counter. I didn't hear the phone ring, but Mac must have. He yelled something at the crowd he'd been talking with and waved his spatula weapon at me.

"Sam," he said too loudly, "that was John Bruger, the bailiff. They want you over at the courthouse right away."

I got up and dropped money on the counter for the coffee. They were all watching me now.

"Thanks, Mac."

Almost every morning there were idlers near the courthouse, some sitting on the walls that bordered its tiny patch of surrounding grass, some standing in the doorways. This morning there were more than idlers. There was a near mob. Some of them were probably the same people I'd seen around the courthouse on other mornings, but some were strangers. There was a similar look to all of them, that look of righteous anger mingled with curiosity, a waiting crowd. I saw no black faces.

The door to the courthouse was closed and John Bob Jenston, one of the deputy sheriffs, was on guard outside it. He grinned at me. "I informed on you," he drawled. "I told the judge you were probably over at Mac's."

He swung the door open and I grinned back and went on in. I had again, for a short moment, that feeling I'd felt so many times before. The courtroom did it to me. It was a big, hollow room and it made you feel small. There were huge windows that ran from three feet above the floor to three feet below the ceiling. Yet even with the windows it was dark. The trees kept out the sunlight, and the fluorescents were somehow absorbed by the ceiling and the drab walls.

Judge Johnson Y. Cleaves nodded to me. "Good morning, Mr. April." He was sitting behind his raised bench and his young-old face revealed nothing.

"Good morning, Judge," I answered softly. "You wanted me?"

He nodded and cleared his throat affectedly. He shuffled through his papers, and we studied each other in that long moment of silence. He was the youngest judge the circuit had ever seen, thirty-seven years old. Not too much older than I. He was, in my estimation, a fair judge. He had, just now, one unfortunate failing, and that was one I could sympathize with: He wanted to be judge again. There was another election coming a year from

November, and the in-fighting had already begun. This was a bad time for a sensational murder to come up, especially the kind of murder where everyone would blame the court for every delay that took place. He was a member of my opposite political faith, but I've never been a fanatic about such things. On the surface, so far, I'd seen little to lead me to believe he let politics influence his court.

He looked down at me and said in his careful, precise voice. "You've probably already heard that a girl named Julia Cunnel was raped and murdered Saturday night or early Sunday morning. They have a man named Alphonse Jones over in jail. I began an initial hearing on him this morning. Some members of his family were here. They indicated that neither he nor they have the money with which to hire him an attorney." He took his right hand and rubbed it along his jaw where a tiny muscle jumped. I'd seen him make the gesture before when he was nervous. He pondered me. "Regular pauper counsel for the county has a conflict. It's my intention to appoint you as Jones's attorney if you'll accept such appointment."

I stood there for a moment thinking. If he appointed me, I'd have to take the job. He was giving me the chance to get off the hook. This was the time to tell him I didn't want it, plead my lack of experience. Somehow I couldn't bring myself to do it. "Your Honor," I said slowly, "I'll take such appointment if it must be given me. However, before I commit myself further, could I talk to Mr. Jones?"

"Of course," he said, and smiled at me. "I'll call the sheriff and tell him to take you over." He reached out his hand and laid it on my arm. "I don't know anything about the evidence in this case and I don't want to know anything more now than I found out in the hearing, but I'll say this to you: It's a great opportunity for you whether you win or lose." He took his hand off my arm. "Don't be hasty in anything you do. The newspapers are going to make a big thing out of this; the Cunnel girl came of a good family and was attractive, and the crime was very brutal. I'll be placed under certain pressures by our citizens and the local newspaper to act quickly, to decide all motions without delay. You have the right to change that by the filing of available motions to remove me from the case. I'm not indicating I want this done, but only suggesting that such change of venue, from the county or from the judge, is available to you."

I searched his face, but it was lacking in expression. He, like my friend Doc Mahoney, would make a good poker player. It was apparent he wanted me to file a motion that would take the case from him as judge. A motion for change of venue would take him off the political hook. And yet I knew, somehow, that he'd not complain if I didn't do it, and that his treatment of me would be just and fair no matter what I did.

He smiled at me suddenly and nodded his head, perhaps reading my mind. "I like this job, Sam. I like it better than being in practice. You're a member of the party that opposes me. After you're appointed there'll be pressure on you also. You can wager on it." He turned away and said over his shoulder. "I'll call Sheriff Tarman for you now."

He opened the door of the courtroom and I followed him out into the hall. There were a lot of people loitering out there. One of them was Dan McGill, the city editor of the local paper. I nodded at him.

He stepped over to us and stood in front of Judge Cleaves and asked in his loud, hoarse voice, "Rumor has it you intend to appoint April here as the attorney for Jones, Judge Cleaves. Is that correct?"

Judge Cleaves stopped and the hall grew silent. "I've not formally appointed him yet, and there's the possibility the prisoner will hire his own counsel or that Mr. April and he will discover a conflict and Mr. April be unable to accept. However, at the present time, under the circumstances as I now understand them, it's my intention to appoint Mr. April if such appointment becomes necessary."

McGill and some others crowded close to me. "What say you about the situation, April?" McGill asked.

I looked down at him. He was quite a bit shorter than me, and his neck was red and puffy below an open Irish face that appeared guileless and understanding. Yet I knew him a little and he wasn't that way at all. He was a member of my own political party, a schemer for power and a practiced liar. He was also a good newsman.

"I've nothing to say at present."

McGill watched me, his gaze going first to me and then to Judge Cleaves, perhaps trying to figure out what had passed between us in the courtroom.

Someone in the background said, "Come on now, Mr. Lawyer. Do you think Jones is guilty?"

I smiled without humor. "I haven't even talked to him yet. I'm going over to the jail to talk to him now."

"Can we get a statement from you when you finish talking to him?" McGill asked.

"If there's anything to make a statement about."

I pushed my way through the group and they made a reluctant path for me. I went down the steps to the lower floor. The sheriff's office was downstairs.

Sheriff Tarman was waiting for me in the hall. He was a big, soft-spoken man who'd been in office for a long time because he knew his job fairly well and never went out of his way to acquire more enemies than were necessary. He shook hands with me limply.

"Judge told me to take you over to the jail," he said. He led me out the door saying nothing more. Some of the newsmen had followed, but more had remained upstairs. The crowd was thicker on the concrete walk between the courthouse and the jail, but no one said anything; they only watched. We went in the outside door of the jail—it was like going from day to sudden night. One single, naked globe burned in the corridor, casting a pale radiance almost devoured by shadows.

The sheriff reached up to a rack and took down a large key, almost as long as his forearm, and unlocked a heavy steel door that opened off a dirty corridor. He went in, and I followed him to a small bare room with steel walls and a door as heavy as the one we'd entered. Using the same key, he unlocked the second door. Behind it was a smaller room.

"I'll leave you here. After I leave and lock, you can call him in here." He smiled. "It's a little better talking here than in the cell block, but you can do as you please. When you're finished talking, ring the buzzer by the door here and I'll let you out. Be sure the prisoner is back in the cell block and that you've closed the door behind him and turned down the lever holding it before you ring. I won't open the door if he's still in the same room with you. The door into the cell block will only open from this side, so make sure you don't shut it behind you if you go inside."

He pointed up on the wall to where a small red light burned. "That light burns only when the door is closed." He turned away and went out, locking the first of the heavy steel doors behind him.

I opened the door and looked into the cell block. There was an old man with gray hair listlessly pushing a worn broom along a dirty, concrete floor. There were two tables, which looked homemade, in the middle of the floor, and above each of them hung a naked light bulb, its cord suspended over bare pipes. There was some urinal art along the lower walls. Higher up, thirty feet or more, there were small, barred portholes. The smell inside was rancid and no air moved. I stepped inside and the floor felt slick under my feet.

I nodded at the gray-haired man. "Will you tell Alphonse Jones that a lawyer would like to see him?"

He stood watching me incuriously for a long moment, saying nothing. Then, without turning his eyes away from me, he yelled, "Jones! Man to see you out here." He bent his head and went back to brooming as if I'd never come in at all. I watched him and saw that he wasn't actually sweeping the floor. He had a cockroach that he'd apparently caught with the broom. It was injured and couldn't crawl quickly enough to evade the bristles, and the man kept turning it with the broom and whispering to it and smiling every once in a while.

A man came out of one of the cubicles to the side of the vaulted room. He was wiping sleep out of his eyes, and when he saw me he hesitated. "You the lawyer man?" he asked. His voice was slow and good.

"That's me," I admitted. "Come out to the outer room, where we can have some privacy."

He walked past me, his step springy. He was a little man, but he gave the impression of tremendous muscular power. Muscles in his arms and neck rippled as he walked. I judged him to be in his early thirties, a light-skinned black. His hair was tinged with red and his features were more white than black.

We went into the small room and I closed the heavy door behind us. There was a wooden bench. I motioned him to sit on it.

"My name's Sam April," I began.

"Where'd you get a name like that? Sounds like a name you'd see on a movie star or something."

"My great-great-grandfather was French. I think the family name was something sounding like April. It got bastardized on his papers when he came through. So I'm Sam April. Judge Cleaves is going to appoint me as your attorney—if you want me. I'm willing, but before either of us makes a decision, may I ask you a few questions?"

He shrugged listlessly.

"Have you hired any other attorney?"

He shook his head.

"Do you, or any of your immediate family, have the funds to pay a lawyer to defend you?"

He shook his head again.

"Maybe there's someone you'd prefer the court to appoint for you other than me?"

He leaned forward on the bench and looked at me; a long searching look, as if he was seeking something in me, in my eyes or face. Whatever it was, I doubted he found it.

He said, "I guess you'll be as good as any in this damned town. I know they're fixing to burn me." He said it casually, as if he were telling an old friend what he'd had for dinner.

"Did you do it?"

"No," he answered softly, and then his voice began to take on weight. "I didn't do it, but they think I did." I could almost see him reasoning the thing out, and it became as if he were talking to himself. "That's enough, ain't it?" he said, his voice dying away. "I mean for them to think it. I'm an ex-con. I've done heavy time. I'm thirty-two years old and I've spent ten of those years in prison. I've been convicted twice, one time for statutory rape after a girl who wanted to do it had her daddy call a cop later. And I got convicted once of armed robbery."

He looked up, including me in his conversation again. "I ain't dumb, Mr. April. I educated myself in prison. I read books, I took correspondence courses. I'm smart enough to know no jury will believe me—not around here." He knuckled his coarse red hair with frustrated, callused hands. "I shouldn't have come back here when I got out, but all my people were here and this was the only place I could get a job so I could get out."

I nodded a listener's nod. "Tell me what happened this weekend."

He looked down at his feet. "I don't remember too

well. Me and my brother, Jeff, we'd been drinking pretty heavy. He went on home and I guess I went to bed. Must have been about eleven. About one o'clock in the morning the sheriff and the city cops came busting into my place and jerked me out of bed. They went picking through everything in the house. They wouldn't tell me what the problem was. I was still pretty drunk and the sheriff got to pushing me around and cussing me. Then a cop came in and he had my hatchet. There was blood on it and he had it laid out on a towel and this cop said he'd found it in my shed."

He clenched his hand. "They kind of took turns pushing me around for a while. Then they brought me on to the jail. I answered them at first when they asked questions, after they read me my Mirandas, but when they kept pushing me and I got a little sober, I also got mad. I quit answering." He rubbed hands over his eyes. "Sheriff's boys didn't stop on me until late." He lifted his loose shirt up. There were welts on his skin, blotching it.

I looked at the welts and something inside me turned over. I kept my voice steady. "If anyone wants to question you again, you tell them that you won't say anything without me being present."

He smiled. "Sheriff Tarman thinks he's tough." He shook his head. "Ain't no one getting nothing out of this man I don't want to tell—not by mashing me around they ain't." He leaned back, taking comfort in that idea. I believed him. There was a toughness to him that Tarman would never have. Nor would I. A toughness born and aged.

"You say it was about eleven when you went to bed?"

"Couldn't have been a lot later than that. I didn't exactly just go to bed. I passed out is more like it. Jeff was gone and I—"

"Who is Jeff again?"

"Jefferson Jones. He's my brother. We was drinking,

but his wife had told him to be home by eleven and he left a few minutes before that, I guess. I finished off the bottle we were working on—there was just a swallow or two left—and laid back on the bed and kind of passed out."

"Did you wake up any time before the police came?"

He squinted his eyes down, thinking. "Maybe I did once, but I was real sodded and I went right back to sleep."

"What was it that woke you?"

He shook his head, not remembering.

"Maybe some noise?" I persisted.

"I don't know."

"Do you know what time it was when whatever it was woke you up?"

"I don't know that either."

"It could be important, so I want you to try remembering. It might make a difference."

He looked at me for a moment, maybe trying. "Nothing in my head," he said.

"OK for now. How about Julia Cunnel? Did you know her?"

"I knew who she was."

"Ever talk to her?"

He smiled a tiny smile. "She never even saw me. She was one of those who wouldn't."

I understood, so I nodded.

"Where do you keep your hatchet?"

"Out in the shed." He shook his head. "I keep it locked most of the time, and it was locked that night. The man who sold me the house gave me the only key. The cop who brought the hatchet in—I heard him say he had to break the lock off the door to get in."

"Did they have a search warrant?"

"They showed me a paper."

"All right. How about this shed? Would there be a way

someone could have gotten in other than by unlocking the door?"

"There's a little window, but I guess it'd be too small for anyone to get in."

"Do you remember the last time you saw the hatchet?"

He looked at me. "I ain't going to lie to you, Mr. April. I used it Saturday afternoon."

I sighed. That shot that one. "OK. This is enough for now. I'll probably be back later today or in the morning. I'm going to talk to some people to see what I can find out about what happened Saturday night. Keep thinking yourself and see if you can remember more about what happened—especially what woke you up." I got up from the bench.

He rose more slowly. "You ain't going to make a deal with them, are you, Mr. April? The other two times I got jail, my lawyers came over here and told me to plead guilty."

"If they offer something, I'll tell you about it. That's my job. If you don't like it and I do, you can ask for another attorney." I smiled at him with a confidence I didn't feel and opened the door back into the jail for him. "Sit tight and wait for me to come back. Say nothing. After I look around, there may be more for us to discuss."

He went on through the door nodding and didn't look back at me. The old gray-haired man who'd called him for me was sitting listlessly at one of the tables under a hanging light. His broom lay in the middle of the floor. There was a dead cockroach beside it. I closed the door on the scene. *Requiescat in pace.*

2

I DIDN'T SAY anything to Sheriff Tarman until we were back in his office. In the courtyard I gave a short statement to the newsmen, led by Dangerous Dan McGill, most of it double-talk about my client's saying he was innocent and my belief in that innocence.

When we got back into his office and closed the door, I did say something.

"Ben, we've been OK with each other since I came here. I'd like it to continue that way." I put my hands on his desk and leaned a little toward him. "One way we can continue to do that is for you to keep your hands and your deputies' hands off Jones."

It took a second for that to soak through. Then his face darkened and he got up heavily from behind his desk and punched a finger in my chest. "Now let me tell you something," he said, breathing angrily. "I've been sheriff or chief deputy sheriff of this county for almost twenty years. No young punk northern lawyer is going to come into my office and tell me how to run my department and its prisoners, especially one that's guilty of a rotten, dirty crime like this one was. Now you haul your butt out of here and don't come sucking around for information or help again—in this case or any other case."

I got mad then too, but I managed to keep it out of my voice. "OK, Sheriff. I'll leave your office and I won't come back without help. When I leave, I'm going to type up a petition to have Jones removed from your jail. I'm also going to have a doctor brought in here to examine him. If the examination shows anything, I'll be with the federal people tomorrow seeing about some rights-violation charges."

He snorted derisively.

"I'm not finished," I said. "If I don't get immediate help, I'll file an action against you myself in federal court and I'll invite all those news people out there in to see me file it. I'll call the NAACP and the ACLU and anyone else I can think of. If I need expert help to keep you from showing what a big man you are, I'll stink around until I get that help. And I'll keep it up until you couldn't be elected head carpetbagger in this town." I opened the door.

"Sam," he called softly.

I closed the door again.

He waved a deprecatory hand in the air and his face seemed suddenly old. "OK. We'll do it your way. I guess my boys and the city boys lost their heads a little. Seeing that poor Cunnel girl with her head beat in and then catching Jones drunk and with that ax all bloody in his shed . . . I wanted—we wanted—to get him to talk, to wrap it up." He nodded his head. "It would have been a big thing for me."

For a moment I felt almost sorry for him. He was the kind of man to whom people were either all good or all bad, and he couldn't help that. As a peace officer he couldn't catch a bear in a telephone booth, but he was okay at serving the legal papers that went through his office, and as far as I knew, he was fairly honest.

"Did it occur to you when he didn't talk that your murderer might be someone other than Jones?"

"He's the one," he said harshly. "He's the one."

"All right. Let's assume, for you, that you're right. A confesssion you beat out of him is completely inadmissible in court."

"I know. We kept working on him and it kept getting

worse. It won't happen anymore. No one will touch him." He grinned at me. He'd recovered normal color. "Forget what I said when I was hot." He punched me lightly on the arm.

I promised I would, but I knew somehow that things wouldn't be the same between us, at least for a time. "Now, can I ask you a few things? First off, where did you find the girl's body in relation to Jones's house?"

"About two hundred yards away. His house is right east of the graveyard. There's a small access road that leads back into the old section of the graveyard which parallels the west side of Jones's house. People visit the newer areas, but hardly anyone uses that road in the daytime except on Memorial Day or Veterans Day or like that. We've been making a run back there nights every once in a while because the high-school kids park back there, but we pretty well got them cleaned out."

"Was she in the middle of the road when you found her?"

"No, she was off to the side. She'd been pulled behind a clump of bushes, but my lights picked her up. I called the city boys and they came on down. You could tell she'd been dragged back of the bushes. Her right heel was scuffed and her other shoe was off and her stockings torn. There was a little blood at the side of the road where we think she got it and more under her head where she'd been dragged."

"How'd you happen to go to Jones's house?"

He spread his hands. "It was a natural assumption. You find a raped, dead girl next to where an ex-con lives, a con with a sex conviction. You then investigate the ex-con. This time we were lucky."

"You're kidding yourself, Ben. No one is stupid enough to kill a girl within a couple hundred yards of his own home, then hide the ax in the one convenient place you were sure to look."

Tarman smiled. "You convince a jury of that and I'll agree with you and them, but I don't think you can do it. Jones was drunk on cheap wine when we came to his house. Besides, he's never been a smart criminal."

"Fingerprints?"

"His were on the ax where the handle was smooth. There weren't any others."

"Was there blood on the ax handle?"

"I didn't see any."

I told myself that what the sheriff was saying was just circumstantial stuff meaning little. Those circumstances could have been used by someone setting Jones up as a probable, someone who knew his habits, knew where he lived. That could be almost anyone in a small town.

"Did Doc Mahoney give you an estimated time of death yet?"

"He thought somewhere around midnight."

"What about Julia Cunnel? Have you checked to see where she was earlier in the evening?"

He waved a hand impatiently. "Don't teach your grandmother to suck eggs. She left home about a quarter to nine, all by herself. Told her mother she was going to the show. There's one that starts about nine and got out Saturday night a bit after eleven. Her house is west of the graveyard, and she sometimes cut through it as the short way home."

I looked at him unbelievingly. "You mean a girl would actually cut through the graveyard rather than go around?"

"Apparently she didn't believe in that kind of crap." He shook his head. "She'd have been better off if she had."

"Was she raped, or had she just had sexual intercourse?"

"Mahoney says she was raped. I don't know much about how they tell for sure, but he said there were torn tissues and, as he said two or three times, some evidence of forcible entry." He smiled at me without humor. "Your man's the one, Sam. Did he remember to tell you he did time for rape once?"

"Statutory rape."

"Reduced from forcible rape."

"He told me," I lied. "The trouble is, Ben, that everyone in town knows his past history. Maybe he got set up for this."

Tarman made a derisive noise. "You're making too much of this. You're trying to turn a simple rape-murder into a complicated plot. Jones was drunk. He saw the girl when she crossed in front of his place. He followed her into the graveyard after getting his ax . . ."

"Then he goes back to his house, locks the ax carefully back up, and peacefully falls into a sodden sleep. It won't scan," I said.

"Ten to one if we'd not found the girl's body right away, he'd have been on his way out of town and into hiding by now."

The phone rang and he turned away from me impatiently and picked it up. There was little sense arguing with him. He could see my logic no better than I could see his, and neither of us was going to find a convert. I got up and went to the door. He hung up and said to my back, "I've always got along pretty good with the coloreds in town, Sam."

I turned back and smiled at him. "Far as I'm concerned, you still do, Ben."

"Thanks," he said. "Last night I felt bad and I didn't sleep good. The only person who'd have been proud of me would have been a Klansman."

"Do we still have those?"

"Maybe. We got some haters whether they wear white robes or not."

I nodded and left.

Outside, the day had turned cloudy again and I felt all of the old fears closing in on me. I went up the stairs to my cubby of an office. In the bottom drawer of my desk I keep a bottle of Jim Beam. I got it out and set it in front of me and eyed it for a time, but I didn't take a drink of it.

The phone rang, bringing me out of the deep black mood and back to the present.

I picked it up. "Sam April," I said.

The voice on the other end was muffled and disguised. "Listen good, you dirty son of a bitch northern shyster. We're going to get Jones. If you pull any crap, some of us have decided we'll get you too. Move on. You won't get any business out of this town. . . ."

I waited for the click of the receiver, but it didn't come. Whoever was on the phone was waiting to hear my reaction. I said, "Instead of just hanging up the receiver, why don't you . . ." I told him where he could place it in lieu of the phone cradle. He didn't do it. He hung up with an outraged bang. I guess I'd hurt his feelings.

I uncapped the bottle. I was starting to get angry. I had a quick one and the stuff ran into me well, taking some of the sting out of the morning. I screwed the cap back on and put the bottle back into its appointed place.

It was well that I did. I'd hardly gotten the drawer closed when my office door opened and in walked two gentlemen whom I knew only slightly. Most people will peck at my door before they open it. These two didn't. Such are the privileges of rank, I guess.

They downed themselves in the two chairs that I have on the other side of my desk. Paul Garran and Dale Willis, the two high dogs of my own particular political affiliation. They were grinning hugely. They looked like they'd been slapping each other's backs all the way down the hall.

"Hello, Paul; Dale."

They glanced at each other, still smiling. Obviously, it

was Paul's place to take the lead. He began by clearing his throat.

"We hear you're going to be Alphonse Jones's attorney," he said, purring about it.

I nodded, looking him over. I'd met him once before at a political picnic—where I went for the free food and a chance to let the locals see the new attorney in town. He'd pumped my hand effusively and told me it was nice to have me around even if I was a damn Yankee. He was a fat man in rumpled clothes who'd run things in the county for some years. You didn't run things the way he did without having some personal iron. There was muscle under the fat, and his movements were graceful for so big a man. He had a deep bass voice and, when necessary, he could give the opposition real hell. He'd done it that day at the party and I'd been impressed.

Now he leaned back in the chair and I heard it creak warningly under him. "It's good to have young lawyers like you coming to our town. Elections are next year and we're going to need a new candidate for prosecutor." He smiled at me wisely. "Someone like you. Even if you aren't from hereabouts, you've got a good war record and you went to a fine law school. And you don't have too many local ties to hurt you. You'd probably be a hell of a vote getter, with some expert help. And that's exactly what Dale here and I are: expert help." He smiled at me wisely again.

"You already have a prosecutor," I said. "Martin Rhinehoff. Last I heard he was planning on running again."

He leaned forward confidentially. "We were thinking of talking Mart into running for judge. That would leave us with an opening. We're wondering if you'd have an interest in the job?"

I waited. The job they were seemingly offering paid four or five times what I was making.

Garran leaned back. "In the meantime there's lots of

other work that Dale and I need done we can keep you busy with. Dale and I are both directors over at the Building and Loan, and we're doing a good amount of mortgage work now. We need a good, bright lawyer to help us get those mortgages out."

I smiled at him. "I'd be happy to help you out with your mortgages, but I thought the Building and Loan had other attorneys for that."

"Leave that to Dale and me." He leaned forward again and we got to it. "Of course you're going to keep Cleaves on the bench for the Jones trial, aren't you?"

"I haven't made up my mind yet."

His sharp, cold eyes looked up at me and narrowed just a little, and I thought he saw me for the first time right at that moment. "We think it'd be a good thing for the party if Cleaves were on the bench for the trial of this case. There's a lawyer from the state capital who's had a lot of experience in these matters we'd like to ask down to help you, show you what motions to file, how to argue them, and so forth."

It became easy to read them. They'd keep Cleaves on the bench and then baste him in their newspaper for every delay I occasioned. With luck the situation could last clear through election time. Yet they had to have me. If they went out and hired their own lawyer to defend Jones, then the scheme weakened because the opposition would probably find out. As far as they were concerned there was nothing wrong with what they were planning. They were only taking advantage of Cleaves's stupidity in offering me the appointment and figuring themselves for smarter politicians than Cleaves was.

"Thank you," I said. "I probably could use some truly expert help when I get into the trial phase of this case. I've never tried a murder case before, and my understanding is that the state plans to ask for the death penalty."

"Then can we assume you'll keep Judge Cleaves on the bench?" Garran asked. He looked over at Dale Willis and they were both smiling again.

I looked down at my watch. Noon. Time to eat; time to meet Doc Mahoney and the other irregulars at the City Club. Besides, I was getting tired of this. I got up from behind my desk. "Gentlemen, I'll do whatever I think will benefit my client most. Before you gentlemen came in, I hadn't made up my mind whether or not I wanted to keep Judge Cleaves, but you gentlemen have helped me make it up."

They smiled collectively.

I continued, "It's my feeling that if I kept Judge Cleaves on the bench for the trial in this case, you'd hurry and harry him and not allow him sufficient time for decision on any motions I might file. That would be detrimental to my client. Therefore, as soon as I'm formally appointed I'm going to file a motion for a change of judge and have a new judge brought in from some adjoining county to try this case."

Garran stood up. His face had gone to below zero. "Is there anything we can do to change your mind?"

"You could have been less clumsy," I said. "With the way the town feels out there right now, if I'd filed the first delaying motion you wanted I couldn't be elected dog-catcher around here. And both of you know it."

His face reddened a trifle. "But the party . . . ," he began in that deep bass.

"The party hell. I don't give half a damn about the party. There's a man's life involved here. There's a town out there already hating him. The man claims he's innocent."

"Bull!" He looked at me curiously. "Just what do you want? What's your price?" He looked around my office. "God knows it looks like you need everything."

I felt my muscles stiffen and they ached to find out just

how much muscle there was back of that fat. I let it go. It was hard, but I let it go.

"I don't want a damned thing from you. And right now I want to go to lunch."

His voice went smooth again. "I'm personally going to make you very sorry."

I nodded. "I'll worry about it."

"I mean really sorry."

I smiled at him. "If you don't get your fat butt out of my chair and haul it out of here, I'm going to make you sorry also."

He flushed. He got to his feet. "Anytime you think you can do it, you can try."

"In exactly thirty seconds I'm going to hop to it."

Dale Willis pulled at Garran's arm and whispered something to him. Garran nodded.

Good old Paul Garran turned away. And good old Dale Willis turned disapprovingly with him. Together they went back through the door they'd so recently opened, impolitely leaving it ajar. I listened for the sound of backslappings down the hall but heard none.

I sat for a moment and wept over lost mortgages and the dream of forty thousand per that prosecutor might have paid if they could have delivered.

Then I went out my office door and to lunch.

I eat every day at the City Club. It's one of the few luxuries I allow myself. Mornings and evenings I usually cook my own meals and complain about the cooking, but come noon I eat out.

The City Club is in one of the town's antebellum buildings. There's a broad flight of stairs that lead up to the dining room and bar. Downstairs there are billiard and card rooms. The wrought-iron rails that lead up the steps to the dining room are old and worn. The double doors at the top take a large, old-fashioned key, so large that I refuse to carry one.

So I buzzed the door, and in a moment it was opened for me by a black waiter. I entered. There's no telephone in the City Club and no clock. If you want to call someone, there's a pay phone outside. If you want to keep track of the time, you carry a watch. Except on Wednesday nights and all day Saturdays, the club is oink-oink stag. Most of the town merchants and professionals belong. Inside they eat and drink, served mostly by smooth, courteous local blacks, who apparently pass the jobs down from generation to generation. But the favorite occupation of the members inside the club is cutting each other up. I don't know how it originally got that way or why it remains so—without murders and assaults—but that's the way it is. Once you entered the door your love life, your sexual habits and equipment, or lack of either, your other physical deviations and mental problems, became open to comment. If you couldn't take it, they'd get on your back and ride so hard you learned to—or quit.

On initiation you were given a large key that opened the door and a key chain with a tiny set of spurs. The key you could do without. The spurs should have been issued larger.

In a way it's a very good club. It has no formal meetings and no officers except a shifting membership committee. Most of the bantering is good-natured, some of it isn't. The food is always good, the drinks excellent. I asked once if any blacks had ever belonged, but got shushed before I did any real damage.

When I walked inside I knew they'd been waiting for me.

"It's Darrence Clarrow," someone quipped.

"Ladies and gentlemen of the jury," someone else yelled.

Three at the bar, none of whom I knew well, chorused in unison: "Innocent! Innocent! Innocent!"

There's a table I almost always sit at to eat. It seats four people. Doc Mahoney, myself, a young dentist, and a real-estate man eat there together. The first to arrive holds it for the others. I looked back. Two of my normal lunch partners were there, but the other two chairs were taken. It could have been a mistake, for I was late. Neither of the two looked up at me. But Old Faithful Mahoney beckoned me from the bar. I got the hint.

I went over to the bar and sat down.

"My hero," Mahoney said softly.

"How come you didn't join the mob?" I asked curiously.

"I've got a cold and can't smell you, despite your faded deodorant." He looked me over and calculated. "I never run with the pack."

I nodded. He made me feel a bit better.

In a moment one of the black waiters brought me a menu and I ordered my lunch. On impulse I had him bring me a martini, although I seldom drink at noon. Mahoney raised his eyebrows when I ordered it.

I drank it down and sat toying with the olive.

Doc leaned toward me and said softly, almost without moving his lips, "You're about to be paged."

Someone touched me on the shoulder. One man, but the rest of the pack watched.

"We need to get the story straight. The word is you've said Jones isn't guilty. What do you base the statement on? Intuition? Guess? Tea leaves?" The questioner was Sid Dart, a tiny man, proud that he was known as one of the sharpest wits in the club. He owned a large department store in town and was also chairman of the board of the big bank.

I smiled down at him. "First off, on the idea that no one is guilty until proven so in this state."

He smiled back at me, but there was a knife in his smile. "Will you lawyers defend anyone, guilty or innocent, for money?"

The whole thing struck me so funny as to be ridiculous. I'd be paid a pittance by the county for defending Jones. I tried to charge fifty dollars an hour for what I did. For pauper work I'd get ten or fifteen. Out of that I'd have to pay office rent, book payments, and the rest.

"Sometimes," I said, "we'll do almost anything we can for money. I'd liken it to a merchant in town near Christmastime. Other times, when we worry on ethics, we go to our bankers for advice. The way we decide is if we don't feel like doing the job and they advise us to go ahead, then we can be sure it's unethical."

He did then what he'd been trying to make me do. He lost his temper. He pointed a tiny finger at my chest, up as high as he could reach. His voice was a scream: "Anyone who'd defend that raping, killing bastard is as bad as he is! We don't need you or your kind around here. And I'll bet I speak for almost everyone."

I said, "Look, you pompous little pimp, your basic problem is they began your last name with the wrong consonant. I didn't ask your invitation to come here and I don't need it to stay." I looked down at him. His face was red and I could tell he was now sorry he'd lost his temper. I doubted he was sorry for what he'd said. He'd probably already said that a dozen times before I came in.

I should have stopped then, but big-mouth Sam couldn't. "It's for sure someone killed Julia Cunnel, but not so sure it was Alphonse Jones. If, by chance, it wasn't him, that means we've got ourselves a murderer running loose on the streets in this town." I looked around the room. "That means maybe all of you gentlemen ought to spend more time watching the wife and kiddies." I looked down at Sid Dart. "Any more questions, whatever your name is?"

He didn't say anything else. I'd made him lose face. He gave me a look full of contempt and hate and walked away. I looked around the room. Suddenly everyone was looking anyplace but at me. The free show was over. What I'd said meant nothing to them. They'd already convicted Jones on rumor and innuendo. No one else could be guilty. The rapist-murderer was in jail and I was an impeder of justice.

Mahoney was smiling. I saw it in the mirror behind the bar. I turned to him.

"That was quite a performance," he said. "I wonder if it was also a smart one?" He looked me over. "Suppose, just to be supposing, that one of the men present or someone they mention it to—and you know they'll tell everyone—is the murderer by some off chance. That makes it open season on Samuel April if you start digging around where no digging's wanted." He shook his head. "I don't know who killed Julia Cunnel, but I do know she's indubitably dead. Isn't your job to get judge and jury to believe Jones innocent and let the cops worry about finding the someone else, if such creature exists?" He watched me with that direct, disturbing stare of his.

"Doc, let me answer your question with a question. If you were operating on a person for appendicitis and you found a tumor growing next to the appendix, you'd cut it out as well, wouldn't you?"

He shook his head impatiently. "That's not the point."

"Perhaps not exactly, but you wouldn't have found the tumor if you'd not performed the appendectomy. Well, I'm into something that makes it so I can't prove the necessity for the appendectomy without suspecting the tumor. In other words I can't, in all probability, prove Jones innocent without maybe finding out who's guilty. I've got to give the trier of fact other options. Or that's how I see it."

He smiled his cynic's smile. "What's all this get Sam April?"

I shrugged. "Nothing, I guess. A little hate that I don't need. Some notice, finally. At least they know who I am today. And I guess whenever there's a barn burning I need to get my hand on the hose."

He nodded noncommittally. "You may have begun a blaze this noon that will give someone, you included, a bad burn. I grew up around here. They used to burn crosses for people like you."

"Let's hope those days are dead. If they aren't, I'll be looking for federal help. Now, tell me what you know that I don't know."

He nodded, willing to do that. "Everyone knew the girl. She played around a little. I've seen her out with some guys." He looked over at me and interest kindled in his eyes. "She used to fool around up in Tarman's office. I never saw them out, but I heard once she was dating our good sheriff."

"How long ago?"

"Seems like a while," he said, looking away. "Probably doesn't mean a thing."

3

BACK IN THE office, after lunch, I dug into the pile of papers on my desk and finally found the jury list. Grand jurors were listed first, then those eligible for petit juror service. The grand-jury list seemed OK. One of the members of the short grand-jury list was even black, something that didn't happen that often. The town was a distance south of Mason-Dixon, and it was one of the towns that had subtly resisted change. The population was about twenty percent black, which wasn't enough for them to run their own candidates, and the several major parties routinely promised the same semi-pro lies every election. There was one black police officer, a couple of black garbage men on the city trucks, and even one black girl working in the welfare department. The black section of town was small. A black could buy elsewhere in town and some few had, but most of those who had moved back "home" eventually. No one burned crosses and there'd been no race trouble in town that I'd ever heard of. It was the kind of town where things were always about ten years behind, maybe twenty.

I called Martin Rhinehoff, the prosecutor. I didn't like him, but I called him anyway.

"Mart, this is Sam April."

He laughed his bray of a laugh over the phone. "I understand you got—shall we politely call it 'the ax'—and have to defend Jones."

"That's right."

"Joy to the world."

"When are you taking it to the grand jury?"

He was silent for a moment. "We're in session now, but probably in the morning."

"OK. I'm hereby requesting that I be notified before you begin presentation of your evidence in Jones's case to the grand jury. It's possible I might want to have Jones brought over to testify. There might be one or two other things. I might also want to question the grand jurors about possible prejudice."

"Well, I doubt we'll get to it until tomorrow morning. And you know there's a black on the jury?"

"I saw that. Congratulations."

"The rules say you should file a formal written motion," he said.

"That's surprising. I thought oral notice was enough." I hesitated a moment. "Well, I'll try to file one this afternoon, but it probably wouldn't get to you anyway, so maybe I'll just wait until morning."

I could almost feel his slippery smile through the receiver. "Up to you."

I hung the phone up. I sat and smiled down at it. There's a rule in the criminal rule book of our state that reads just as the prosecutor had said. To parade a defendant in front of a grand jury, a request must be made in writing. In reading advance sheets I'd come on an exception to the rules. If the defendant was charged with a felony involving the death penalty, then oral request, such as I'd just made to Rhinehoff, was enough. If I knew Mart, he'd try to get all he needed from the grand jury this afternoon or evening and think it was a good joke or lesson for me. That would suit me fine.

I doubted the wisdom of having Jones testify before the grand jury. Grand juries are prosecutors' creatures. Barring any member's having a personal prejudice against Jones, I had no desire to have any of the grand jury stricken from the panel. But I could use the delay that failure to notify me would bring—if Rhinehoff wanted to engage in sharp practice.

For a time I sat thinking at my desk. Assuming—for the sake of believing in what my client had told me—that Jones hadn't killed Julia Cunnel, I had then to assume that there must be another circumstance in which she'd been killed. One could be that some sex deviate had followed her from the show or known her route. Happenstance could almost be disregarded because of the locked shed. The using of the "inaccessible" ax ruled it out.

Another idea seemed more likely: Jones had been set up for this thing, either by someone who hated him—which might or might not be probable—or, even more likely, by someone who had reason to kill Julia Cunnel. That meant planning; planning to commit the crime and make it appear Jones had done it. It further meant planning with a knowledge of both people.

I decided to find out, for starters, if anyone benefited monetarily or otherwise from Julia Cunnel's death.

I got up and paced the small floor of my office. I wasn't a detective. I had no real training to be one. And I had no funds to hire a detective—and neither did Jones. That left it up to me. I remembered the faces in the City Club. Some of those faces had once been friendly to me. Now that was gone until this was over. If I'd accepted the appointment and laughed about it and gone along with their ideas, then I could still have been one of the boys; a northern one, but still mostly OK. By not so doing I'd become part of something about which the town felt compulsive hate. Some of that hate would rub off on me, because after Jones was gone, I'd be a visible symbol for him. Whether I won or lost, the hate would remain.

Sixty or seventy years before, the town would have done what Mac and his customers had undoubtedly discussed this morning while I drank my coffee. They'd have lynched Jones. Now, even if I proved him innocent, part of the town would always believe I'd gotten him off with slick lawyer's tricks.

I'd fare better only if I came up with the killer.

The town lay out there beyond my office door.

Waiting.

Anything I did was certain to be wrong.

The scars on my chest ached. I rubbed my hands together, but no heat came, even though the afternoon was hot and it was humid in my office.

The phone rang. It was Judge Cleaves. "I've appointed you. I just signed the entry on it."

I thanked him and hung up.

I went on out of the office, locking the door behind me. If someone wanted to see me, they'd have to come back tomorrow.

The street was an oven. There was very little breeze and the bright summer sun beat down. Very few other pedestrians were foolish enough to be out in it. I walked down three blocks to my apartment. I keep my car there and walk to work. It saves gas and parking meter money and keeps the belly flat.

Jones had said something about his brother's being with him that night. I figured a logical place for me to start was with that brother.

I drove my beat-up ten-year-old Chevy down into the black area of town. I thought I knew where Little Al Jones's place was, because I'd been initiated in the rites of the nearby graveyard by one of the local belles one late night not too long before, and the sheriff had said that Jones's house was the last one before you got to said graveyard. I even knew about the patrol that came through, because the girl had been very careful about where we parked and walked that night.

I parked near where two black men were standing on the street talking. They were watching Jones's house. Both of them wore coats and ties, despite the weather.

I asked them where Jefferson Jones lived. They told me distrustfully and watched me in the same fashion as I walked away. It was, they said, around the corner.

I backed up and parked in front of the house they'd described. There was an old, shredded tree in front that lightning had failed to kill. There was a tire full of flowers underneath it, the only bright thing in the eroded yard. Near the tire there was a dirty lounge chair, empty now. The house behind had needed painting ten years before, not gotten it, and now was disintegrating. It was a shotgun frame, probably three or four rooms, with running water when it rained.

I went up the walk, if you could call it that. I knocked on the decomposing screen door. Somewhere in the rear of the house I could hear something. In a moment a man came to the door.

"You Jefferson Jones?"

He watched me out of reserved eyes. He nodded finally.

"My name's Sam April. I'm your brother's attorney."

He thawed a little. He opened the door and shook my hand shyly, enfolding it in his soft, big paw. "Glad to meet you."

"I'd like to talk to you about what happened Saturday night."

He nodded and smiled, flashing perfect white teeth. "Come in," he said. "Mrs. Garran just brought us some stuff, but she'll be leaving soon."

The practice of law teaches you to seek attitudes—nuances—in a voice. I sought one in his, but was unable to identify it.

"Who?" I asked.

He looked at me, but I couldn't read his eyes. "Mrs.

Garran. She comes here now and then. Mostly when there's trouble." He opened the door and I followed him in. The room was hotter than outside, despite the fierce sun. The furniture was faded and overstuffed, of a style known years ago as Midwest modern. I sat down gingerly and looked over the prints on the walls and the carefully arranged clay statues on a whatnot.

A woman came out of the back of the house. She was white. Jefferson Jones looked over at her and nodded at me. I stood up.

"This is Mr. April, Mrs. Garran," he said awkwardly. "He's the lawyer who'll be defending my brother."

I nodded at her. "Mrs. Paul Garran?"

"Yes," she said. "Do you know my husband?"

"We're slightly acquainted."

She moved a bit toward me and into the light from the open door. She wasn't a big woman and she wasn't old, but she gave the illusion of both size and age. She was smartly dressed. As she moved I became positive she was also wearing a girdle—a no-nonsense one. Her movements were quick, but they seemed restricted.

I saw that she was appraising me also. "I guess you can do the job, Mr. April." She moved a step closer. "There are some of us around here who are sympathetic to the black plight, which is, I feel, one of the most needful of causes. I'm happy to count a young lawyer like you among those people." She smiled a warm, large smile. "They need you. Alphonse needs you. I certainly hope you'll be able to talk a jury into finding Alphonse not guilty of this awful murder-rape thing."

I nodded, unsure of what to say.

She turned to Jefferson, dismissing me. "I'll be back sometime soon. If anyone needs anything, you've only to call." She turned away and marched to the front door, where she picked up a gaily colored basket and carried it out with her.

The room seemed bigger when she was gone.

"How about a beer?" Jefferson asked, obviously as relieved as I.

I debated for two seconds. "Thanks, I will."

Bourbon in the morning, a martini at lunch, and now beer. Samuel April, budding alcoholic.

He was gone for a while. When he came back, he had two Miller Lites in his hands. I took one of them gratefully.

"What was that about?" I asked, waving at the door Mrs. Garran had left by.

He shrugged. "She's on the board of the local black movement. She's big in several state and national organizations. Anything happens, she's on your doorstep."

I nodded and put her out of my mind for the time being.

"You were with Al at his place on Saturday night?"

"Yes. I came home just before eleven. Lin—that's my wife—goes to work at eleven and I take her. She's down at her mother's now or she'd tell you the same."

"I believe you. What shape was Al in when you left his house?"

"He was flying." He nodded. "He'd smoked some pot and he'd drunk a bunch of wine."

"Did you see anyone when you left and went home?"

He thought about it for a long moment. "No, but that doesn't mean anything. The trees and bushes block out the road." He stretched out in his chair and took a swallow of beer. I tested mine also and we smiled companionably at each other. It was cold and good. "Only person I saw on the way home was old Mrs. Calling, and she wasn't in the cemetery. She was sitting up on her porch when I went past. Leastways, I think it was her. I couldn't see anything for certain, because her porch was dark, but I could hear her in her rocking chair."

"Where does she live in relation to Al's house?"

"First house east of him." He took another swallow of his beer. "She's got the cancer and she's had all sorts of things done to her and none of it helping. She don't sleep much." He smiled with the pity of the living for the dying. "She's going to die soon, I guess." He nodded his head. "Doctor Mahoney's car's parked out there in front of her house lots."

"Who'd Al pal around with?"

He looked surprised. "He knew them all and was friendly enough with most of them except when he was crossed."

"He have any enemies you know of?"

He shook his head. "Maybe Mr. Mont. His daughter was the one got Al sent up before. Cops and Mont came looking for her when she didn't go home and caught her and Al in the bushes and she started screaming rape."

"That was the rape charge?"

He grinned. "It wasn't no real rape. She was sixteen, so they had Al on that and he pled out. But it wasn't no forcible rape even if they did charge it. You could look at that little piece and she'd fall over backward and beat you to the floor. She was born with her pants at half-mast. Al got unlucky. If Mont had looked earlier, he could have caught almost anyone in the neighborhood."

"That helps some," I said. "From the way I heard it I thought maybe he'd forced the girl." I thought for another moment and had another taste of the beer. "Who was Al working for?"

"He worked days for Mr. Garran. Then sometimes, when he'd get done, he'd garden for anyone who wanted him. Al's got a green thumb."

"You mean Paul Garran?" I asked, feeling like a stuck record.

He nodded. "Mr. Garran's a big political wheel, and

he and Mrs. Garran helped Al to get out of prison. Part of it was Mr. Garran had to promise Al a job down at his feed mill."

"How long's he been working for Mr. Garran?"

"A few months. Ever since he got out of prison."

I thought for a moment, taking another drink of beer in the process. Jefferson Jones finished his and sat the aluminum can regretfully on the floor.

"Did you ever see Mr. Garran down at Al's house?"

He shook his head. "I don't think so. Maybe right at first, when Mr. Garran sold him the place."

I rolled with that punch also. "Al bought his house from Garran?"

He nodded. "When Mr. Garran got Al out of prison, he sold the house to him on contract and he was taking so much a week out of Al's pay for it."

I leaned toward him. "Think hard for me. Have you seen anyone around the place where Al lives, anyone out of the ordinary, anything at all you can remember?"

He shook his head.

"Is there anyone you can send me to who might help me?"

He tried. He thought for a long time.

Finally he shook his head again.

I got up from the chair. "Thanks a lot for talking to me. If you hear of anything or think of anything that might help, you come to my office or call me."

"You're going to help him, aren't you, Mr. April?"

"I hope."

"He didn't kill that girl. Al wouldn't kill anyone. He never would even hunt when we were kids, and he's never been able to stand seeing anything dead. He never did like to fight, so he made himself strong so he'd not have to. The only time he will fight is when someone gets him real mad. Most of the time he just likes to sit around with a book." He thought for a moment. "He was real, bad drunk that night."

I nodded.

"I was uptown this morning and I heard what they was saying. They're going to give him the death penalty. Mrs. Garran said they couldn't, not without a fair trial, but I know they will. They'll give him all the 'fair' trial he wants and then they'll give him the electric chair."

I touched him on the shoulder. He was a big man, but his hands seemed soft and he had a beer belly.

"You have a job, Jeff?"

"Not now. Not for quite a while. But Lin works."

His wife could do the work for the family. Yet I liked him.

"They're not going to do that if I can help it, Jeff."

He grinned; defeat moved a little beyond his line of sight.

I left.

4

MRS. CALLING'S HOUSE was neat and bright. There were little shrubs at the corners of the house and a geometrically correct flowerbed. I went up the weeded brick walk. The porch was shadowed, but I could see the form of a woman rocking there.

"Are you Mrs. Calling?"

She leaned forward in the rocking chair. "You can come on up to the porch and out of the heat."

I came on up. There was no other chair, so I sat down gingerly on the front banister of the porch.

She wasn't terribly old, but she was sick. The skin hung off her stick arms, and her dress had been doubled over sharply and was cinched in by a belt with extra holes drilled in it. Her night-black face was thin and there were deep pain lines around her eyes. She rocked back and forth slowly in the chair, watching me. If the body seemed ready for a mortician, the eyes, framed inside the pain lines, were not. They were alive and strong, looking out on the minute world they saw with unquenched curiosity.

"I'm Amanda Calling," she said. Her voice was soft and raspy. "You're Samuel April."

I must have looked surprised. She held out a book. "This book has everyone's license in it. When you turned up there and went to Jefferson Jones's house, I checked out your number." She smiled a small smile. "That's how I knew." She looked out at her yard. "I'm a nosy old woman, Mr. April. My neighbors will tell you that, and I agree with them." She nodded her head. "Being nosy is one of the few things I do of interest anymore."

"Jefferson Jones said you were up here on your porch when he went past your house Saturday night. Is that right?"

She looked at me oddly. "Did he say that?" She tapped her stick leg with a restless hand. "He must have been soberer than I thought he was. He was about as quiet as a truck going past. His wife's a good woman, but Jefferson ain't much."

"What time did you go to bed?" I asked, smiling.

She thought it over for a moment. "Maybe midnight or a little before, but I didn't go to sleep for a long time after that." Her voice was composed, but her eyes suddenly weren't. "I'm not sleeping well these days." She looked at me with an almost religious fanaticism. "I've got cancer. I've had radiation and chemotherapy, and Doctor Mahoney is going to operate on me soon. He's my very good friend."

"He's a friend of mine too," I said.

I don't think she heard me. She was living the day when she'd be well again. She ran her hands over her thin face, smiled and nodded her head. "I'll be better then," she said, believing it.

For a moment I found myself unable to look at her, because I was sure my eyes would mirror my disbelief. I looked instead out into the yard.

"This is a nice place you have here, Mrs. Calling."

"Thank you. Would you like to see my garden in the backyard?"

"When we're done I'd enjoy it."

She nodded and waited patiently.

"Did anyone else go by that night after Jefferson passed your place?"

"No." Her eyes lost contact with mine. "No, I didn't see anyone else."

I'd developed a feeling for lies. I could be fooled and not know it, but not often. This woman couldn't fool me. She was not telling me the truth. I decided to try something else.

"How about the car?"

Her eyes came up quickly and they were frightened. "What car?"

"The one that went past that night into the graveyard."

Her voice was uncertain. "I didn't tell the police when they asked. I'd drifted off a little. The pills do it. I'm not really sure if one went past. And I don't want to get into this problem." Her eyes pleaded with me. "I won't get into trouble because I didn't say anything at first and now I am, will I?"

I shook my head.

"It was real dark. I couldn't even say what color or make it was. It was gone and past before I could get woke up." She looked at me, and I still saw fear in her eyes and knew I hadn't gotten all of it. "Who told you about the car?"

"Alphonse," I lied. "Did it stop in the cemetery?"

She remained hesitant. "What did he say?"

"He wasn't sure."

Her voice gained strength. "I guess it went on through then."

"It never came back out your way?"

"No. It went on through and probably out one of the other two exits. It never came back."

"And you didn't see anything?"

Again a small hesitation. "No."

"How about Alphonse Jones? Did you hear anything from his house after Jefferson Jones went past yours?"

She rocked her chair back and forth. "My best estimate is that I went into my house sometime before twelve o'clock. From this porch and from my bedroom you can't see Alphonse's house at all, or hear anything from it very well. And that's what happened. I didn't see anything or hear anything after I went inside."

"That seems to do it," I said, getting up and dusting the seat of my pants. "Unless you can think of anything else?"

She shook her head and smiled. "Now, can I show you my garden?"

I nodded.

We walked around the corner of the house and I saw the dogs. She had a runway for them in the backyard with one of those little doorways, hinged, that could be opened for them to enter her house. The opening was closed now. The dogs were big Doberman pinschers, and they strained toward me and slathered ferociously at the wire fence that restrained them. What made them most frightening was that they didn't bark.

"Down, lads, down," she ordered softly. They moved back a little, still eyeing me. "I've trained them not to make a fuss," she said. "I can't stand a noisy dog."

One of the dogs left the fence and went to the hinged opening. "Sometimes at night I let them in. They like that," she said.

We moved on. The east side of her backyard had been walled. There was a garden there. Flowers grew in careful summer profusion. If there was a single weed, I didn't see it.

"If I ever build a house," I said, "I'm coming to you for advice on the garden."

She smiled, pleased. "That's the nicest thing anyone's said to me in a long time."

She pointed over at the pen where the two big dogs still patrolled. "There's my true friends," she said. She walked back and I followed, staying a few steps behind.

43

She reached in and they licked her hands through the wire, forgot me for the moment, and began to frisk.

"They'd try to tear you or anyone else up who touched me—except Doctor Mahoney." She touched their noses with small fingers and bent to whisper secrets to them. "The doctor's stolen them from me. Dogs know their friends, Mr. April. The doctor's been very good to them. He brings them steak bones." She bent to them again and went on talking baby talk.

I took advantage of her preoccupation and looked over at Al's house. It was visible from behind Mrs. Calling's, and the side of it was only about twenty or thirty feet from the side of hers. I could see Al's shed too. The door hung open now. Al's house itself was not much more than a tarpaper shack.

I moved a step closer to Mrs. Calling and she turned.

"Thank you for showing me your garden."

"Stay and talk a little while."

"I'd truly like to, but there are places I have to go."

"Are you very busy then?"

"Yes," I lied. "Thank you for talking to me. I'll come back again soon."

I walked on out toward the front of the house. Across the asphalt road, near my car, quarrelsome birds fought over the remnants of some popcorn someone had spilled. The two old black men who'd told me where to find Jefferson sat morosely in the shade watching both the birds and me, still suspicious. I gunned my Chevy down to the front of Al's house.

The house looked even shabbier from close up. The front door was slightly open, the porch crumbling. On the east side the porch had given up the fight and sagged far down toward eventual breeding with the earth close below. I went in the door. The inside was filled with a few old pieces of junk furniture. The walls had acne of the plaster. From the east window you could see the windowless side of the Calling house, but you couldn't see her front porch. The west window, on the other side of Al's house, was broken and boarded up. Through cracks in the boards you could see the cemetery property line, where cultivated bushes began to grow and marble monuments rose. From either window the shed was out of view.

I spent a while looking, but there was nothing much to see. There were a few wine bottles near the unmade bed. The sun through the window cut a swath in the grime of the floor.

The neighborhood was silent. Being in the house made me moody. It seemed alone and waiting. I went out the back door. Mrs. Calling had gone inside. Her dogs scrambled to the fence, threatening me again.

Al's shed was open and I could see where the lock had been forced from the door. There was a broken window on the side. I arm-measured it. A small child could have squeezed through it, perhaps, but it would have been tight going.

I checked the screws that held the lock to the door. They were dull and rusty. If a screwdriver had been applied to them in the past few days, there was no evidence to show it.

Inside, the shed was oddly clean. There were a few well-worn gardening tools. There was a single bale of hay in one corner, so old now that it had lost its smell and one of the wires holding it together had rusted through. There were some marks on the side of it—small and deeper brown than the yellow of the hay—that might be blood. They were in line with the window.

I went back outside and took another good look at the lock itself. It wasn't an expensive one and it seemed to me it wouldn't be impossible to pick.

Mrs. Calling's back door was now slightly open and I thought she was watching me. I waved, but she didn't wave back.

I drove on down through the graveyard and found the other two exits Mrs. Calling had spoken about. One of them exited to the state highway. There was a street lamp above it. I stopped the car and got out and looked up curiously at the light. It seemed unbroken.

The other exit was on the main street of the town. Across from it the neon sign on a restaurant flickered, and on the opposite corner was a gasoline station. I checked the Chevy's fuel indicator. It was almost over to empty. I drove in for ten dollars' worth of unleaded.

The attendant was Billy Nugent, a guy I knew. He'd been in the office once or twice with family troubles.

I pulled the hood release and got out. He put the gas into the tank, grinning at me.

"Why don't you try our super no-lead in this heap sometimes?" He screwed the gas cap back on and went around to lift the hood.

"I've got it weaned. It won't run on anything with higher octane than your bad unleaded. If I put high-test in it, the cylinders would come up through the floorboard and beat me to death."

He pulled the stick out of the oil. He wiped it against an oily rag, examined it critically, and put it back in. He took it out and examined it again, then replaced it, satisfied.

"Okay," he said.

"What time do you close, Billy?"

He interrupted spraying water on the windshield. "Two in the morning."

"Are you on every afternoon and night?"

"Yep. I work from three in the afternoon till I close. My brother works the other shift."

"Did you see anyone coming out of the graveyard late Saturday night?"

He eyed me shrewdly. "No. That don't mean that someone couldn't have come out of that entrance over there without me seeing them. But I probably would if it was late. I been listening to the radio and hearing the talk and I'd imagine you're interested in after twelve and there wasn't anybody I remember." He leered pleasantly. "If it was lovers, most of them have moved out to the lake once they started patrolling the graveyard. And someone could have gone in and me not seen them, because when they enter the lights don't shine over here."

I nodded and got back in the car, and he finished wiping my window with a flourish. I paid him and he wrote it on a cash ticket, so I could set off part of the cost, however minute, to Uncle Sam.

He leaned confidentially against the car window. "Everything's just fine at home now. Instead of drinking it up in the taverns, I take my beer home and Jean helps me drink it. She's put on five pounds from beer and lack of worry."

"I'll bet she looks better," I said. His wife had sued him for a dissolution of marriage, commonly called a divorce, and I'd delayed things until she quit listening to her mother and they'd reconciled.

"I've still got my fingers crossed, Mr. April. Her mother calls her every day and I see her car drive past here lots."

I smiled. "Stick with it. And call me Sam. Even the courthouse wino bums do. My friends might as well."

He smiled back. "I used to see that gal that got killed, Julia Cunnel, hanging around the bars some. She'd have guys with her, but I don't remember who now."

"If you hear anything, let me know," I said.

He nodded.

I drove away feeling pretty good. It was nice having at least one other guy besides Doc who still liked me.

I drove down by the river and parked there for a time. There's nothing like an evening river to calm you. The river runs smooth and deep and forever. Just sitting and watching it took some of the kinks out. There were lots of boats out, and some kids on water skis cut the water up into sharp-breaking lines.

One of the difficulties with being a lawyer is an inability to divorce yourself from the problems of a client. Ethically, if such is humanly possible, you need to believe what they tell you and thereafter seek the rest of the truth. You're your clients' advocate. Many times you must take this with a grain of salt, sometimes with a whole box in criminal cases.

For now I believed Jones. I needed no salt. I'd convinced myself he wasn't guilty. The whole thing seemed to me to be too pat and stupid.

Even if I'd convinced myself, I wondered whether I'd ever be able to convince anyone else. Even if I found another possible killer, it might be like mountain climbing. I could pick a trail up, and when I got to the top I could yell down to the people below about what I'd done and what I'd found. What I wondered was if anyone would hear me. They'd only see the mountain, not the trail I'd made climbing it.

Jones was in jail and accused of murder. Because that had happened, it was easy enough to see him as the murderer. Somewhere, in the shadows outside the jail, secure now, there had to be someone else.

I rubbed my hands over my eyes, trying for clearer vision.

It was time to go back to the jail and see Jones again, but I decided to put it off until morning. I wanted time to think over things, private time.

I started the car and drove on up the river. It was starting to cool off a little and the hills on the other side of the water had taken on their evening purple look. My chest began to ache again, and for the thousandth time I thought I ought to quit here and go someplace where it was always hot and dry; Arizona, maybe. But even in a couple of years you can put down roots. I'd come because I'd seen this town and liked it. I'd come to put away old memories, to begin again.

Even though my chest ached, I knew my problem wasn't medical.

I parked in front of the old, run-down house where I keep my bachelor apartment, if you can call a room with a kitchenette and bath an apartment. At least it had a private entrance, on the side of the rambling house. My landlady, who lived in the major part of the house, was a nice person to rent from. Increasing age had stilled some of her urge to pry and deafness decayed her ability to sense my improprieties.

My side of the yard had a little cobbled walk that led back to my door and then on to a larger apartment behind mine, which was vacant now. The walk was shaded by magnolias, and a large rambler rose climbed the side of the house near my door.

There was something pinned to my door today. It was a note. It was on the letterhead of M. & J. Adjusting Co.

The note asked me to please come to the country club and contact a Mr. Louis as soon as I arrived home.

I got back into my car and drove out to the country club. It's not a particularly exclusive place. Membership can be had for a few thousand a year by any white Protestant. It's even slightly less for bachelor members. However, I couldn't have raised what they wanted in order to enter the kingdom of heaven. But I'd been there for meetings and parties.

My Chevy looked out of place among all the Caddies,

Mercedes, and Lincolns. I left the keys in it, assuming no one would have bad taste enough to steal it. Some dowagers and kids were sporting in the chemically blue water of the swimming pool. Someone, who must have mistaken me for a member, waved gaily at me and I waved gaily back.

I walked in the imposing front door. A black waiter hurried over to me, knowing I wasn't genuine and privileged.

"A Mr. Louis is supposed to be waiting for me."

He nodded, reassured. I followed him back past tableclothed tables with candles on them.

Mr. Louis was obese. He was drinking martinis and he was undoubtedly a man born to the country-club tradition. At least he dismissed the waiter well and gave him a munificent dollar.

His voice was an unexpected high tenor. "Ah, Mr. April, I've been to your office at least three times this afternoon. I drove down from the capital to see you after calling the dean of your old law school."

I nodded. "I was out of the office on business."

"Would you care for a drink?"

"Thank you. I'll have a Scotch and water."

He beckoned the waiter again and ordered it. He lowered his voice confidentially. "I'm claims superintendent with M. and J. We're looking for a good man to take over a new territory in the northern part of the state. Your law-school dean thought you might be interested. We pay pretty well and we're trying, these days, to hire lawyers who've had some trial experience."

I leaned forward. "How much do you pay?"

He smiled. "We'd start you at thirty-five a year, with some guaranteed raises to forty-five within three years, stock options, a medical plan, and a company retirement plan. In addition we'd furnish you a new car and pay all travel expenses and whatever moving expenses you'd have from here."

Thirty-five thousand a year was a lot more than what I'd make here. "How soon would you want me to go to work?"

"Very soon. I'm hoping you'd not have anything here you couldn't farm out to someone else. Our man we sent up there six months ago quit to go with another company and we need someone now."

I was tempted. Cleaves would let me off the hook.

I looked at the fat man and he looked back at me and smiled. The thought suddenly came to me about how he came to be in the country club. Someone in town must have vouched for him.

"Stay and have dinner with me," he said. "We can discuss this."

I knew I was looking a gift horse in the mouth, but somehow I couldn't help it. "There's a call I need to make first. I'll use the phone in the bar."

He nodded politely and I went to the bar, gave the bartender a five-dollar bill, and used the phone. After calling information and forking over a handful of change, I called the dean of my old law school. I must have caught him at dinner.

"Who is this?" he asked severely. I remembered his temper had never been too even.

"This is Sam April."

"Who?"

"Sam April."

"Then God damn it, who's Sam April?"

I hung the phone up. I looked in at Mr. Louis. The waiter was back and he was ordering dinner for both of us, employer-employee style. I walked back out the front door of the country club. It appeared that if Mr. Garran couldn't buy me one way, he was going to try another.

I decided I could buy my own dinner.

5

I LOOKED AT the girl who sat on the other side of the booth with real appreciation. She'd finished her steak and pushed the plate back. I hadn't eaten all of mine, but I was done.

"So you've been had, Sam." It was a statement.

She was Jan Gale, who worked for Dan McGill at the local paper, and I knew she'd probably trailed me to Otto's Bar and Grille to pump me, but I didn't feel too bad about it. You couldn't look at Jan Gale very long and feel bad about anything.

"I don't feel like getting appointed to defend a man is getting had."

She looked at me shrewdly out of uptilted blue eyes. She was a tall blond with a body that could light a candle at fifty yards. She should have been winning beauty contests instead of working on a newspaper. And though I'd seen her appreciatively before, this was the first time we'd looked at each other with mutual—I hoped—approval.

"Who else do you think the judge could have gotten to take the appointment?" she asked innocently.

"He can appoint anyone he wants," I said a bit stiffly.

"In theory, yes. But this is a cruel world. No one in his party would willingly have taken the job. His regular contract pauper counsel turned it down. With the feeling there is about Jones in this town, he'd have been biting the hands that he wants to feed him if he'd appointed anyone else." She looked at me and smiled. "Then, if he'd appointed anyone else from your party, he'd have been left on the bench and my paper would have screamed early trial and generally burnt him at the stake while the lawyer representing Jones added fuel to the fire." Her voice went casual. "Now my opinion is that you're going to take him off the hook by asking for a change of judge."

"Just how heavy is your paper in with the party?"

"Heavy enough," she said seriously. "Oh, I suppose if they caught one of our own people with his hand illegally in the till, they'd do something about it, but it's a strong, politically partisan newspaper."

I waved at the bartender for two more beers. Otto's is dark and quiet and a little shabby, but the food is good and the beer is cold. It's not the country club. They don't bother with oil paintings on the wall or redecorating every other year, and the bartender hadn't been to Yale, but it suits me and I ate there as often as I could afford it.

I reached out and touched Jan's hand with the tip of my index finger. "Did Garran or Willis send you down here to try to talk me out of that change of judge?"

She stiffened a little and a hint of steel came into her eyes. "No one sent me here. I came, partly for myself, partly for the paper. I'm trying to figure out what makes you tick. I know about the change of judge thing because Paul Garran was in McGill's office this afternoon and I could hear them yelling at each other in there. Then they made calls all over the state, trying to figure some way to get you out of the case." She looked at me and shook her head with a touch of wonderment and sadness. "You've killed yourself with the organization and with the paper. I guess you know that."

"How does one kill himself with a newspaper?"

"They'll cut you up every way they can. If you win a case, they'll ignore it. If you lose, it'll be three columns, boxed, on the front page. You're not going to be able to make it in this town now, Sam." Her eyes seemed sorry about it.

"I'm staying," I said.

"Why are you here at all? The way I hear it, you were born up in one of those wholesome states that begins with an *I* and wandered in here a couple of years ago. Why?"

"Lots of reasons. The best is I drove through here once a few years back on the way to Florida. I was going down easy, away from the interstates. I saw the town and liked what I saw. I remembered it when I needed a change."

"And now you can't stay," she said.

"I'm staying," I said again.

She hadn't taken her hand away and my fingers were still there against it. I could feel that small current you can't fail to recognize run through me.

The waiter brought more beer and she took her hand away.

"You know," she said softly, "you can't go through life the way you're doing."

"What is it I'm doing?"

"Not swimming with the stream. Being a loner and an outsider when you're already a loner and outsider."

"Politics isn't one of the things I care about, Jan." I poured some of the cold beer into my glass.

"If you care about anything, it doesn't show much. You're mostly northern smart-ass." She looked down at her misty glass and made absent finger drawings on it. Her fingers were long and exquisitely shaped. Watching did things to me. I wondered if she could see that?

"Someone hurt you badly," she said, guessing.

I leaned back and kept my face carefully blank. "All kinds of things have hurt me—women, wars, practicing law."

She nodded. "And right now you think you can get

away from hurt by being hard and smart-ass, but don't you realize that in this case you're laying yourself open for the biggest hurt of all? What's going to become of Sam April's faith when they strap something you do believe in in that frying chair up at the state prison?"

"That's something I don't think they'll ever get done," I said. I then added, without irritation, "Let's get off me and back to the murder. I'm a man badly in need of information, and maybe you can supply it."

She sighed. "I will if I can. And that means if I have the information and am at liberty to give it out."

"Fair enough." I toyed with my beer glass. "Do you have a morgue at the paper?"

She nodded. "A good one."

I asked hesitantly. "Can someone not in the good graces of the paper look through it?"

"Right now, if you want," she said obligingly.

"Finish your beer and then we'll go on down."

She examined me with interest. "What are you looking for?"

"Just looking right now. No real reason. It's just that I feel that the answer to this thing is wrapped up in people, local people, and your morgue might tell me something about those people."

She drank another sip of beer. "I'm ready."

"Fine. Let's take a look."

We got up and I paid the waiter, over her protests.

The newspaper office was only a few blocks from Otto's and the night air was cool and fine. It was good to have her beside me. She had a long step and she easily kept pace with me. We didn't talk on the way to the newspaper office.

I had her dig out files for me and I read them through while she watched.

There was one on Julia Cunnel, which was pitifully slim. Her sole entry was a high-school graduation picture, the eyes already big and lost and seeking. Then I asked Jan to get me the files on Paul Garran and wife, Al Jones, Jefferson Jones, Doc Mahoney, and Mrs. Calling.

There was nothing of overwhelming interest in the files. In Garran's there was a yellowed clipping of his marriage, from the capital paper. Mrs. Garran had been a nurse before he married her. The later stuff in his envelope was an assortment of appointments and political triumphs. His wife's was much the same. Memberships and drives, most of them as a black sympathizer. A march on a courthouse in the sixties, a picture of her looking out from a jail cell, where she'd been sent by an unknowing judge.

Doc Mahoney's file showed individualism. Once he'd been sued for assault by an herb healer whose nose he'd broken in a street altercation. Another time, probably when he was suddenly taken drunk, he'd used his car to plow up a group of parking meters near his office. He must have worked out both, because there was no follow-up story on either.

Alphonse Jones's folder had stories about his two major convictions, along with smaller stories about a host of minor ones, while his brother Jeff's contained a tiny marriage story and the write-up of an arrest for public intoxication. Amanda Calling had once built a spite fence between herself and a belligerent neighbor. There was a photo of the fence and a younger, heavier Mrs. Calling standing defensively beside it. I noticed that the fence was neatly built.

Jan sat at her desk and watched me impatiently.

I was soon done. I stuffed the clippings back into their respective envelopes and handed all back to her.

She laid them on her desk. "If you think I'm not going to go through those again in the morning, you're wrong."

"You won't find out any more than I did. So far those are the people I've run onto who might be concerned in the murder. I had a professor in law school who used to say that if you want to find an answer to why something happened, the best way is to check the people involved in the happening." I looked at the small pile of envelopes with their clippings. "Those undoubtedly aren't all the people involved in this thing. There are more. But somewhere there's a reason why the Cunnel girl died—greed, fright, love, panic, hate."

"And you're sure that someone killed the Cunnel girl and set Al Jones up for the police?"

I sat down next to her desk and kicked my feet up on it. "No. I'm giving it a strong maybe. And maybe something I read or hear might give me a hint. If I can dig out the reason, then maybe I can find out who done it. And I've got to rely on me alone because no one else is looking. I'm the only one thinks Jones didn't kill that girl. He's too smart and the thing doesn't fit in with anything else he's ever done or what I know about him."

"You really believe that in spite of the evidence?"

"No. I believe it because of the evidence. Or lack of evidence."

She shook her head. "Sam, you're a screwball." She smiled to take the sting out of it.

The telephone on her desk rang. It was an unexpected, even eerie sound in the dim light of the office. Jan reached for the receiver.

I could hear a voice on the other end of the telephone, but I couldn't make out what that voice was saying. Jan murmured sounds into the speaker and made squiggles on a yellow pad in front of her. In a few moments she put the receiver back on the hook.

"This may interest you," she said softly. "The grand jury just returned an indictment against your client for murder, felony murder, with a separate page asking for the death penalty." She watched me, and I didn't know whether there was contempt or sorrow in her eyes.

"Why weren't you up there at the courthouse protecting your client instead of sitting around hatching up smoke suspects?"

I smiled. "There are more tricks to my trade than meet the immediate eyes. I take it that your caller was Martin Rhinehoff?"

She shook her head. "You know I can't tell you that."

I tried to look hurt, but didn't do a good job of it.

She waited.

"All this," I said, "is getting us nowhere. I'm not selling you on my side and I don't really know enough to do it. So instead of trying further, how about taking my car and going out to the Oasis for a tall, cool one?"

She watched me out of sheltered eyes.

"But don't try any funny stuff," I said. "My mother wanted me to save myself for marriage."

"I was just about to say something like that."

"Prude."

"But I'd about decided not to," she continued.

I smiled at her. "You don't know me well at all. For all you know, I may be the town's secret sex fiend. I may take you out and rape and murder you."

She smiled back. Just watching that smile sent my temperature up five degrees.

"I hope you're not that drastic," she said.

We went out into the night. She locked the newspaper office door behind us.

My car was on a side street, up through the alley. We walked together, now hand and hand. Neither of us said anything and the heavy asphalt of the alley absorbed our footsteps. There was no noise at all.

The side street where I'd parked my car was well lighted. A policeman stood beside the Chevy, busily writing up a ticket for me. It was a guy I knew. His name was Jim Lary.

"What's the problem, Jim?"

He handed me the ticket silently, almost apologetically. His eyes wouldn't meet mine. "You're parked more than eighteen inches from the curb. I measured."

I looked up and down the street. I was parked in about the same manner as all of the other cars. None of them had tickets.

"You going to ticket the rest of them?" I asked.

He still avoided my eyes. "I'm off duty in five more minutes, so I won't have time." He turned away.

We drove on out to the Oasis, neither of us saying much. We went in and took a booth in the dim interior. There were a couple of kids dancing, well glued, to the music that came out of an old-fashioned jukebox. They were good, and we drank and watched them.

Jan tilted her Tom Collins back. "End of being a privileged character for Sam April."

I nodded. "If I pay it, the ticket's only a couple of bucks."

"I've seen them sit on people before," she said. "You don't dance when they play the tune and you become a second-class citizen."

A little anger burned uncomfortably in me, but it was small so far and could be contained. I smiled at her and it wasn't a lot of effort to make my facial muscles relax. "Jim Lary wasn't doing it on his own. Somebody told him to watch for my car."

She was quiet for a moment, and then she reached out and touched my hand. "You're right and you're wrong, Sam. But mostly you're just alone." Her eyes watched me. "Maybe all I've got is a feeling for the underdog, but I'll help you if I can."

We watched the dancers and after a while joined them.

The Oasis is an old roadhouse. Periodically, Tarman or the state boys would raid it and close it. On Saturday nights the waiters wore roller skates and the place served only beer and wine and simple mixed drinks. Order a

Zombie or something and they'd toss you out on your can. But this was a Monday. I'd been in the place once on a Saturday, but it had been too much for me. Now I came only through the week. Why they wore skates on Saturday I'd never been able to figure, but they did. The Saturday night I'd been there we'd had to park almost a quarter of a mile away and the inside had been jammed with drunks and people trying to catch up with them. There'd been one of those hillbilly bands. I liked the jukebox and the customers of Monday much better.

After a while, it got late. We finished our drinks and went to the car.

There was a touch of moisture in the air and the Chevy liked it. Its motor purred along and Jan moved beside me, her eyes half-shut. A few miles from downtown, but still within the city limits, the road inclines down and there's a pull-off spot. From it you can see the river and at night it shines with reflected light, making the town seem like an insignificant adjunct. The moon was hanging above and the trees on the far side seemed without color, yet substantial and alive. I eased into the spot and let the motor idle. She sat up and looked at me.

I watched the river. I didn't look at her. "I was married once, Jan," I said softly. "Sometime I'm going to tell you about that, but not tonight."

She considered what I'd said silently.

I watched the river. It was clean and good from this distance. Perhaps it might wash some of my problems away.

She leaned over against me, soft and fragrant. One hand touched mine and her voice was hesitant. "If you stopped here to kiss me," she said, "please go ahead."

I had enough presence of mind to turn off the motor.

I kissed her and it seemed warm and right and good. I could feel her body tighten against mine, but it was me who pulled away.

She was breathing heavily and so was I.

"I liked that," she said softly. "I'd like a lot more." She drew away a little more at the look in my eyes. "But not tonight." She moved close again. "Kiss me once more and then take me home."

I kissed her again—a long kiss.

I didn't feel tired. I felt wide awake.

The spotlight came on then.

They must have pulled up behind us to watch. The light glared off the mirror and into our eyes. Jan gave a startled little sound beside me.

The man who came to the window was Police Chief Spotts. He leaned authoritatively up against my window.

"Get out your license," he said. He looked at me without recognition in his eyes, though I talked with him almost every day.

I took my wallet out and found the license and handed it to him. Jan had moved over close to me, but my body hid hers and I was sure he'd not seen her face.

He looked at me. "You're parked within ten feet of the highway right-of-way. And you smell like a distillery." He looked down at my license. "Get out of the car."

I opened the door and got out.

"Walk the white line at the edge of the highway."

I nodded. "Watch this, Jan," I called. I went to the edge of the road and walked the line, but Spotts wasn't watching. He had his flashlight on Jan's face. I came back.

"Am I under arrest?" I looked at him and at the police car. The other policeman in the car wasn't looking at me. His eyes were down, hidden.

"You should be," he said, not certain about it anymore.

"That isn't what I asked. I want to know if I'm under arrest."

He stepped back from me. "We'll let this one go. I'll give you a break this one time."

I moved after him. "Better not try again, Chiefie." I

reached in my pocket and pulled out the parking ticket. I tore it into small pieces and let it flutter in the night breeze. "Fix that for me, will you?"

He looked down at the bits of torn ticket and then at me. His eyes were full of hate.

"Better call him, Spotts. Tell him I don't scare. One more ticket, one more harassment, and I'm going to do my best to smash you all. And we won't try it here. We'll try it in federal court. You tell Garran that I'll subpoena him and I'll subpoena every damned one of your officers. We'll see who breaks and tells why you put the heat on. Some of them might lie for you and Garran, but I don't think all of them will perjure themselves. And then we'll see how easy you walk after I take your hat, ass, and overcoat on a civil-rights charge."

He was now in full retreat. He jerked open the door of the police car. "You got it wrong," he said.

I shook my head. "I've got it right. Let me alone and let me do my job." I nodded at the other officer. "Drive on."

I went back to the Chevy and got in, and Jan and I watched the taillights of the police car diminish down the road. I was trembling. Jan touched my hand and we sat for a long time, saying nothing. I didn't feel triumphant. I felt drained. I felt like Al must have felt when they came for him.

Jan pulled away finally and reached down and turned the key on and nodded at me.

I took her home.

6

I DREAMED.

The bed was soft, but every once in a while I would half-awaken. In between, I dreamed.

They were dropping hydrogen bombs all around me and I could feel the heat on my face. I was running and running, but there wasn't any place to hide. There was a shadow man in a dark coat after me, his face always averted. Sometimes I'd try to see that face, and once I almost caught a glimpse, became sure, then became the pursuer and ran after him in a sea of slime and hotness that impeded every step. Then they dropped the final bomb and this time the heat was all around me and a part of me and I was burning.

I awoke.

I was sweating. It was the darkest part of the night outside my apartment window. I lit a match and looked at my watch. It was almost five in the morning. I worked things through in my head again. Someplace there was someone, perhaps someone that I knew nothing about yet, but there was someone. And I'd find him if they'd let me. Finally I drifted back into a deep, dreamless sleep. When I awoke again it was a more reasonable hour, almost eight o'clock, and the sun was my friend outside my window.

At nine o'clock the sheriff took me to the jail to see Jones.

He looked as if he'd slept better than I had.

"You look like hell, Mr. Lawyer," he said.

I grinned at him. "If you'd said I looked good, I'd have slugged you for lying to me."

He rubbed hands over his eyes and up through his almost red hair. There was something akin to admiration in his eyes. "They say someone tried to arrest you last night."

"Who told you that?"

"They put a drunk in here last night, and they must have picked him up right after your problem with them. They were talking about it and he wasn't as drunk as they thought he was."

He fell silent and I looked at him carefully. "Sheriff or his people haven't been bothering you any more, have they?"

"No. He was around in the cells for a while last night." He smiled. "He treated me like I was his grandmother."

"What's bothering you, then?"

"I'm causing you lots of trouble."

"Let me worry about my troubles."

He nodded, reassured somehow.

"I'm short on time," I said. "I'll send over a motion for you to sign. Read it and sign it."

"Sure," he said.

"There's a couple of things I want to ask you again now that you've had time to think. First off, can you think of any enemies you've made, people who'd go out of their way to see you dead or in jail for a long time?"

He grinned a tough grin. "There's the sheriff and the prosecutor. . . ." He watched my face, and when I didn't grin back he sat thinking for a long moment. "I don't think so," he said finally.

"How about this Mont whose daughter you got caught with?"

He shrugged. "He hasn't guts enough to kill his own flies. He hates me bad enough all right, but he was scared to even sign the affidavit. His wife finally made him. Besides, he must be close to eighty years old."

"How about Paul Garran?" I asked slowly. "You worked for him, he owned your house. Did you get along all right with him?"

"Sure. OK."

"Have you been working for him ever since you got released from prison?"

He leaned forward on the bench and his voice was slow, as if he was trying to make sure his words conveyed exactly what he was feeling. "Mr. Garran got me out of prison. I know he did it for other reasons than just me. But if he hadn't given me a job up front, then the parole board would have turned me down." He looked at me. "I ain't never busted my butt much for anyone in my life, but I'd bust it for Mr. Garran. He and his wife treated me fine. Put me in that house cheap. She even kept me in food until I could get on my feet. Mr. Garran came over yesterday and wanted to hire me a lawyer, but I told him you were my lawyer. I know there ain't no chance, no real chance, but I told him I knew you'd try." His voice was earnest. "He said he'd get me a good one if I could get you to quit, but that it'd have to be that way. Otherwise people around here would yell politics."

"Do you want me to quit?"

He looked down at the floor. For a while I wasn't sure what he was going to say.

His voice, when it came, was so low I almost didn't hear it. "No," he said. "No, I want you to stay. I can hear the town out there. Maybe you're my only chance to live."

I put my hand on his shoulder; the muscles were bunched and tight. I didn't think there was any good reason to tell him exactly why Paul Garran wanted to be rid of me. I said, "I'd have quit yesterday, but I can't quit now. I think you're innocent."

He looked up at me and I saw something in his eyes I'd not seen before.

It was hope.

I'd put it there and maybe I shouldn't have done it. The deck was still stacked and I was drawing at a pair of threes with a pat hand sitting on the other side of the table.

"Did you remember anything more about waking up?" I asked.

He shook his head.

"How about a car? Did you hear a car?"

"I don't know. Maybe."

"Could that have been what woke you up?"

He shook his head, not knowing. "Let me think on it some more."

After a while I let him go back inside. I buzzed the sheriff.

We went back together out into the other world beyond the jailhouse door.

The crowd had thinned out some this morning, but they were meaner and angrier than they'd been the day before. The curiosity seekers had vanished and their places had been taken by the rabble that invades every small town when a rape-murder, black-white crime takes place.

There was a small cluster of them against the courthouse wall and I heard someone mutter something about a "jackleg lawyer" when I went past. Another one spit close to my shoe. I stopped then and the sheriff stopped, too.

He said without force, "Now let's not have any trouble, Sam."

"Better move these douche bags out of here, Ben," I said, but there was no need to say it. They'd already begun to dissolve around the corner of the building. The one who'd laid one near my shoe started to say something and I moved a step closer to him, within range, but he must have seen the others moving away. He turned and ran to join them. Tarman and I went on up the steps and into the courthouse.

Tarman smiled an amused smile. "If you hadn't done that, I might have had to arrest that one for spitting on the sidewalk. It don't seem necessary now."

He walked into his office and I followed behind and closed the door.

I hadn't won the small encounter outside, that I knew. By noon the story would be around that someone had spit in my face and made me take it, and the man in the mob outside would be the day's hero.

I'd be a bum, just as I'd always been.

Tarman sat down behind his desk, ruffled papers, and watched me curiously.

I put my hands down on his desk and leaned down. "In checking, I keep getting the word that you knew Julia Cunnel, Ben. That you'd taken her out."

His eyes came up to mine and he nodded finally. "I don't know where you found out and I only hope my wife never does." He got up from behind the desk and went to the window. "I was a damned fool. Always have been about women. She was young and she kept asking for it. I've got kids that aren't much younger than she is—was."

"Where were you about midnight the night she was killed, before you made your run through the graveyard?"

He looked at me, and comprehension came into his eyes. "Why, Sam, I believe you suspect little old me. I ought to be angry, but I can't afford to be. Bob Jenston was with me here in the office and left only about five minutes before I made the run. In fact I dropped him off at his house on the way to the graveyard." He tapped a finger on the windowsill. "She was a sweet kid, Sam. I got the feeling, with me, that she was experimenting. She wasn't really interested in me. She wasn't pressuring me to leave my wife or anything." He waved a hand in the air. "Check with Bob. He'll back me on the time. And she'd been dead for a while when I got there. Doc will tell you that. Then go blow it around town that I was taking her out. Maybe it'll buy me some of your heat."

"I thought we knew each other better than that, Ben."

He looked me in the eyes. His face had gone taut as he'd talked. Slowly it began to relax. "Sure," he said. "I'm sorry I said that."

I went on over to the door and opened it. I nodded good-bye and Tarman nodded back halfheartedly.

Deputy Jenston was just coming in the back door. He confirmed Tarman's story, which was no surprise. I thought Ben Tarman might kill, but only when the law allowed it.

I went on upstairs to the county clerk's office, fighting off a newspaperman or two on the way. Calla Simon, the court stenographer, was in the clerk's office filing papers. She was a little, dumpy girl with an engaging smile and a mind as sharp as a switchblade. She was in her far thirties now, and she'd apparently given up on her early hopes of marriage. She liked to drink and have a good time, and several times we'd done the town together. She could talk on anything and she knew more about skeletons in respective local closets than the undertaker and had heard more confessions than the area bishop. I signaled her I wanted to talk.

She sidled up to the counter. "Good morning, Brother Beam," she said in her harsh, crisp voice.

"How about going over to your office for some talk?"

She nodded. "Wait a minute and I'll get us a couple cups of coffee."

She turned away and went into the clerk's vault. They

kept a coffeepot brewing in there all day. In a minute she was back with two steaming cups.

We walked on over to her office. It was tiny, with room for her desk and chair and one other chair. We sat and sipped coffee in the hot morning.

"You're looking lovely this morning," I began.

She sighed gustily. "You didn't come in here to romance me. I hear you and Jan Gale were out last night and that our local gendarmes tried to waylay you. If you were with Jan, I know I'm now outclassed. So state your business."

I leaned toward her. "Tell me what you know about Julia Cunnel?"

She smiled, and it gave an oddly appealing look to her plain face. She said, "Julie was okay. I knew her pretty well when she was working for Sanders. As far as I've heard, she wasn't taking the boys on in droves, but she was interested. I don't know about any enemies. But we weren't close since she left Sanders. She used to like money—I mean to dream on it, plan on it."

"You say she wasn't taking them on in droves. Who was she dating recently?"

She hesitated, and I knew she was probably thinking about Ben Tarman but that a loyalty to him greater than her liking for me stopped her from naming him.

"You know Ken Cavin?" she asked.

"No."

"Drives around in a jazzed-up Mustang convertible. She was going with him up until recently. I heard they broke up." She eyed me, and there came a touch of malice in her voice. "He also used to go with Jan Gale."

I nodded. "Where does he work?"

"Works down at Haysma's Garage. He's a very pretty boy." She tapped her forehead. "Not a ton up here, but lots of beautiful muscle."

I digested that. Calla had a mind like an autumn squirrel and her accurate sources of information included the police force, the sheriff's office, and innumerable other people she exchanged information with. She could read a local pedigree four generations backward.

"How about Paul Garran?"

She ran her tongue over her lips and pursed her mouth. "Well, he's on the opposite side of the political fence and I suppose I'm prejudiced because of it, but I don't like or trust the man or his wife. They say they've done a lot for some people, but I've found the same people have done a lot for them. She hangs around down in blacktown all the time with a flower basket on her arms. Why's she do that? Black people got the same rights as the rest of us and they don't need her. I've heard some of them say it." She shook her head. "If I guessed at her reason, I'd come up filthy. With those looks, maybe she and her beloved have a problem. He's tough and a fanatic as far as his party is concerned." She gave me a smug look. "If he had any true ability to see things, he'd belong to our party rather than yours."

I smiled at her. We'd long ago decided there was enough local difference between the parties to make an argument.

"Have you ever heard about either of them doing any running around?"

She hesitated. "Other than the nasty rumors I help spread about why she hangs out down in blacktown, I have to say no. And he's a stout fellow at the church and Masonic meetings. I think he'd figure he was being really risqué if he watched an R-rated movie. I'm suspicious of men like Garran. Maybe he ain't hunting because he wouldn't know what to do with it if he found it. Like a dog chasing cars."

"How about Sanders, Julia's onetime boss? Could she

have known something about Garran by working in Sanders's office and around his files?"

She thought about it. "There you might have something. Sanders used to do Garran's legal work, did it until maybe a year before he died. Then things blew up. Garran got Sanders kicked out as attorney for the Building and Loan. Right after that Sanders sued him. It was an auto accident case. I'll look it up the next time I get a chance. I know they quit speaking. Sanders won the case and Garran had to dig in his own pocket for some of the judgment because he didn't have enough insurance. It really galled him. He reported Sanders to the disciplinary people at the state bar, but nothing came of that, because the accident was after Sanders quit representing him." She looked up at me and nodded. "Sometimes you can tell about people by the way they drive their cars. Garran's got a heavy foot and it got him in trouble then and might again sometime."

Something came to me. Julia Cunnel was dead and so was Sanders. "How did Sanders die?"

"That was odd," she said softly. "I don't think what happened means a blessed thing, but you can check it if you want. Sanders lived out in the country, had a big farm out there. He had a man worked for him days, but at nights he was alone. He had a heart condition, but it mustn't have been too bad or my guess is his doctors would have made him move back to town. I knew he was supposed to avoid excitement and overwork because he told me once. One night Billy Mishak, one of the state troopers, saw a light back there about four in the morning, so he drove in to investigate. He found Sanders on the front porch. All the lights in the house were on, even the lights near the barn and the gate lights—as if he'd been expecting someone." She looked up at me.

"Or maybe had seen someone outside?" I added.

She nodded. "It gets curiouser. There was a shotgun beside Sanders and one barrel of it had been fired through the front window. He was dead of a heart attack."

"Any signs of anyone else being around?"

She smiled. "Mishak told me he checked, but the ground was so hard it hadn't taken any tracks. He thought maybe a dog or even a wolf had come into the front yard and tried to get into the house."

"Wolf?"

She nodded. "People say there are still wolves around here. Ask any farmer. My bet is that they're wild dogs running loose and not wolves."

"Or maybe someone who hated Sanders and knew he had a bad heart . . ." My mind worked at turning the story over and over. I felt a new excitement rising in me.

"Give it up," she said. "In his business Sanders didn't make the kind of enemies that want to kill. A lot of people were glad when he got dead, but my bet is no one helped it along. Besides, a few weeks before he died, he and Garran made up. Shook hands in public down at the Elks. Besides, who'd want to kill Julia Cunnel too?"

"How long did she work for Sanders before he died?"

"'A year or two maybe."

"How about money? Did she have any?"

Calla shook her head. "Someone was up from the county treasurer's office collecting money for flowers. Apparently there was one small insurance policy and it won't be enough to bury her. Her folks are doing that."

I got up. She'd given me enough to chew on for a while. "Calla," I said, "you are a pearl without price. One more question and I'm out of your hair. How did Julia get along with her family?"

"I guess OK." She spread her hands. "I'm sure they tried to hold her down." She was silent for a long moment, frowning at her hands. Then she suddenly looked up at me. "Say, did you see last night's daily disappointment?"

"The local newspaper? No."

"Well, you've been excoriated. They had you on the front page and the editorial page. I heard around that Garran was in your office yesterday. You must have told him you were going to get a change of judge."

"I did. You can tell the judge I'll file the motion in the morning. Have you got a copy of the paper?"

"Sure." She reached into a drawer and brought it out. She watched me curiously as I read it.

I skimmed the story on page one. In it I was referred to as "an inexperienced, young attorney who'd only moved into the legal ranks of the city a few months ago from a northern state." Most of the story was about Jones. It recited his previous convictions, except that statutory rape was shortened to rape. The story was slanted to leave no doubt in the reader's mind that Jones was guilty. All the reader was left to expect was conviction and execution. It did get in one other dig at me; something Jan had led me to expect. It closed by saying, "April's only other previous local case of note here was a jury trial in the *Malcolm Williams v. State* trial. Williams is now serving a two-year sentence at a state prison on a check charge. In that case, Mr. April was also appointed by the court."

The editorial was meaner. It was entitled "Legal Machinations." It recounted how shady lawyers could delay and frustrate the orderly workings of law, and hinted that the town might very well see an example of this in the Jones case. It didn't mention my name. I thought I could see the fine hand of my bar brother Rhinehoff in the legal language. It was possibly libelous, possibly not.

There was a picture of me on the editorial page. The caption read simply: *Samuel April, appointed by Judge*

Johnson Y. Cleaves to be attorney for Alphonse Jones in the brutal Cunnel murder case. See story, page 1. I didn't like my picture. They must have taken it just as I had exited the jailhouse door and was squinting at the sun. I looked sly and dirty, as if I'd just thought up some new trick to hamper the orderly workings of justice.

Calla was still watching me as I laid the paper down, but I kept my face impassive.

I asked, "When you read this, Calla, did it make you think Alphonse Jones killed Julia Cunnel?"

"I wouldn't believe that paper if it said the sun would come up tomorrow."

"Thanks for the information. I owe you one double Scotch, which I'll pay at your convenience."

"Stick around," she said. "We'll chew the fat some more."

"That sounds appetizing, but I'll take a rain check. I've got other fat to chew."

7

I DROVE PAST Haysma's Garage, but Ken Cavin wasn't there. I was told he lived by the lake near Doplin. I drove on out.

I spotted the cabin by seeing the car. It was a red Mustang convertible with flames on the fenders and *Ken* in small white letters under the driver's side window.

A bare-chested boy-man was polishing it.

I parked my car off the side of the road and stood looking at the lake for a moment. A few fishermen's boats rowed on the calm waters. I'd been out to the lake before. It was the "fun" place for those who didn't belong to the country club. On Saturday nights it was something more. Then, you couldn't hear the frogs for the heavy breathing and you couldn't kick at a bush without getting kicked back for your pains. The man at the pavilion did a brisk business on Sundays in bootleg whiskey and prophylactics for those who still used them. However, the aficionados claimed it was more private than the first and fifth greens at the country club, also noted sexual watering places.

The boy polishing the Mustang didn't look up until I was close to him.

"Are you Ken Cavin?"

He nodded his head cautiously, as if afraid of ruffling his carefully combed hair. He was a tall boy, very well made. He was deeply tanned and his face was almost pretty, marred only by a thin, scraggly mustache.

"My name's Sam April. I'm a lawyer."

The mustache curled a little and I thought he'd heard the name. "So?"

"I hear around you knew Julia Cunnel pretty well. I'd like to talk to you about her."

He shook his head. "Haven't got the time or the inclination. Buzz off." He turned back to the car.

"Suit yourself," I said to his back. "I'll serve you with a subpoena then and see you in court."

He turned toward me and moved a step closer. There was quick rage in his eyes. He said, "Don't do that to me, Mister Lawyer. I wouldn't like it." His fists were closed tight and he looked around to see if anyone was watching us.

I smiled gently at him. I'd lost most of my combative urge around the age of twenty, along with a tooth. "Don't be tough, bud," I said. "Maybe you can take me, maybe not. Before you get the job done I'll bet I can make that profile of yours a lot more interesting. And I'll still drop a subpoena on you, whether you win or not."

He scowled and turned away again. He opened the door of the red car and ran his hand caressingly over the wheel.

"Do you call her Christine?" I asked.

He shook his head, not comprehending. "What is it you want to know?"

There was a tree stump behind me. I let my hands relax and went over to it, inspected for splinters, and sat down. "I hear you dated her."

He nodded. "Up until a month or so ago." He smiled. "She had the hots for me."

I semisuccessfully fought my curling lip. "What ended this big romance?"

He waved a deprecating hand. "I just got tired of her. She was always pushing at me, trying to reform me." He scoured an invisible speck in the bright red paint. "I like lots of room."

"Who'd she date after you dropped her?"

He shrugged his shoulders without real interest, but his eyes came up to mine and I saw knowledge there his shoulders had declined. "One of the boys told me he saw her out in the capital one night with some guy there."

"Who?"

He shrugged his shoulders again and this time his eyes concurred. "You might check Doc Mahoney. I hear he took her out once or twice."

"Where were you the night she was killed?"

"Around town."

"Did you see her?"

He hesitated and then nodded. "I saw her at the show. I asked her if she'd like a ride home." He grinned. "For old time's sake. She didn't take me up on it. I guess she should have."

"What time was that?"

"Sometime after eleven. When the show got out. We talked for a moment."

"And then did you follow her?"

"No."

"You ever been in any trouble?"

"No." His eyes came up to mine again and this time I couldn't read them.

"What'd you do after you couldn't pick her up?"

"I drove around some, looking to see who was on the street." He nodded at me. "Man, I hate this town. There's never anyone around. There wasn't nothin' that night either."

I looked at him and didn't like him much. Maybe that was my fault and not his. He had about as much depth as an August creek and he appeared slightly more intelligent than a trained chimpanzee. Maybe the dumb act was put on for me. He could have done it. He had motive and opportunity. But he was out and Jones was in.

I got up from the stump and his eyes narrowed. "Hang around," he said. "I got some beer in the trunk."

I shook my head. All heat at first, now all smiles.

Maybe it was the idea that I constituted some kind of authority and he was trying to ingratiate himself with me.

I went back to the Chevy and we scorned his polished Mustang by kicking dust on it as we drove away.

I found State Trooper Billy Mishak at home. I knew where he lived. It was out in one of the new subdivisions in a house that had once been neat and now was beginning to look beat-up after only three or four years. I hoped he'd be off duty.

He was. I caught him in his garden, hoeing out weeds around tomato plants that looked as if they needed both fertilizer and rain. Mishak was wearing loafers and an old pair of Levis. There were two kids playing in a battered swing in the backyard. They were blond, like Mishak.

We shook hands. Once, he'd been a witness in a reckless-driving case I'd lost in city court. He was a tall, serious boy who'd already put in a lot of years as a good state cop. We'd always gotten along.

"I'd like to talk to you for a few minutes if you can spare me the time."

He nodded. "Come on in the house and sit down and have a beer."

We went into a clean kitchen and he opened one for me. "Can't have one myself just now. I go on patrol in a couple of hours." He grinned amiably. "If I had a beer, sure as hell I'd pick up some guy and he'd swear I was drunk."

"Or his lawyer would," I said, grinning back.

His eyes went serious. "I hear stories about you, Sam."

I waited.

He continued. "If they ever get the chance, there's some locals who are going to shove it to you."

"Even after last night?"

He nodded. "Especially after last night. You can bet it won't be that crude next time. They can afford to sit back and wait. They'll most probably leave you alone now until after the trial. Then they'll try to make it look like someone else did it." His eyes met mine and conveyed the message he didn't approve of the plans. "Forewarned is forearmed, some bright guy said." He dismissed the matter with a wave. "Now, what do you want to know?"

"Remember the night that Sanders died? I checked and found out you made the run. Can you tell me about it?"

He nodded. "I guess I can. There wasn't a lot to it. I was coming down State Road 508 and there wasn't much traffic at that time. It was about four in the morning. I'd been up and back that particular stretch of road maybe half a dozen times earlier that night and never seen any lights over at Sanders's place. Maybe they were on before and I didn't notice them, but I don't think so. Traffic was light and I think I'd have seen them." He shook his head.

"Anyway, there were lights on back at his place. I knew he lived alone and I'd heard he had some heart trouble, so I drove on in. I could see him when I got into the driveway. All the lights were on, even the ones in the outbuildings you could turn on from inside the house. He had on an old nightshirt and he was face down on his steps. He was maybe half an hour dead when I checked him. He'd fired one shot from a double-barreled twenty-gauge shotgun through his own front window. The shotgun was beside him. There was an unfired shell in the other chamber. I took the shell out and checked it and the gun. He'd tried to fire it, but the firing pin was bent or the shell was defective. Anyway, it never went off."

"Did you check the yard?"

"Sure," he said. "There wasn't a thing, but that was maybe because the ground was hard. Hadn't been any rain for maybe two weeks. Someone could have come in and he could have fired the shotgun at whoever it was. There wasn't any stock or poultry missing the next day when the hired man checked, and I did have him check. It could be Mr. Sanders just thought he saw something out there in his yard. Maybe he was already starting to have his attack and he just got some kind of illusion in his head that there was someone or something out there. So he gets his gun, gets more excited, and then shoots through his own window. Then he runs outside and that finishes him off." He nodded, trying it on for size.

"I suppose it could have been that way," I prompted.

"It was funny, Sam. You expect a guy that's died to have an expression on his face. I've seen everything from smiles to grimaces. But I never saw a face like the one on Sanders. He looked like he was insane with anger." He looked up at me, puzzled. "Maybe he was mad at dying like that."

I nodded. "Anything else you can think of?"

"Yeah. Tell me why you're so interested in Sanders and the way he died."

I took a long swallow of the beer he'd given me. "I'm not for sure. I guess I'm just stabbing in the dark and trying to get ideas. Julia Cunnel worked for Sanders. She's dead and he's dead. It looked like something for me to check on."

"You mean because of the Jones case?"

"Yeah."

"You got yourself a tough road there." He leaned back in his chair. "I wouldn't have your job. Not only in this case, but in all of them." He rubbed his eyes with his hands. "People are no damned good. You put them on the witness stand and they'll lie every time it affects them and theirs. Your man Jones is a chronic. I wouldn't put a lot of faith in anything he said."

I smiled. "You mean he doesn't tell the truth to police officers?"

He got my point and grinned back. "You know what I mean," he said. "It's not only him, but damned near any one of them."

I snapped my fingers. "Say," I said. "There's something else you might be able to tell me. Do you know Ken Cavin?"

He grimaced. "I know him."

"Has he ever been in any trouble?"

He nodded. "Mostly minor stuff—except one time. He almost killed another kid with a knife at one of the local dives one night. The kid he punctured refused to file charges."

"He told me he'd never been in any trouble," I mused.

He grinned again. "That's what I told you. They all lie."

That started us and we swapped some experiences about other people who'd lied to us and in a while his wife came back from the grocery with a sack of food. She was a tall woman with a pleasant face. He introduced me and I talked with them for a few minutes more, thanked him for the information, and then left.

I went back to my office and laboriously, on my tired typewriter, prepared a motion for change of judge and then took it over to Tarman to give Jones.

After I left Tarman's office I went through the judgment dockets in the clerk's office looking for cases in which Sanders had been the attorney and where he could have raised heat and maybe made the kind of enemy I was seeking. I went back three years, hoping it wouldn't have happened before that time and knowing Julia Cunnel hadn't worked for Sanders that long. Sanders had been a fairly busy attorney. Checking him out took the rest of the afternoon. There seemed to be nothing of interest other than the Garran case. Most of Sanders's work had been probate plus a few mortgage foreclosures he'd filed when he had the building-and-loan business.

Two years ago he'd filed a personal-injury suit against Garran and there was a released judgment on record, which meant the judgment had been paid. It was for sixty thousand dollars. If Garran had been forced to kick in partly out of his own pocket, I wondered how much.

I thought about it. If I assumed I was right and there was a rapist-killer who'd been able to disguise an earlier murder or maybe more than one and get away with it/them, then it became logical to suspect someone in an official capacity or someone close to the system, who knew how it worked. I knew enough about both the coroner's job and the sheriff's job to realize they'd usually be pushed for time, willing to accept obvious solutions. For example, if the sheriff found an old man dead, he'd suspect what had killed him would be what he suffered from—heart trouble. Doc Mahoney would be aware of every bad heart in town. Someone like Doc or Tarman, who knew how crudely things were done, might very well be my killer. But so might anyone else smart enough to see the shortcomings in the local system of investigation.

Like Paul Garran. Like Ken Cavin, if he was putting on an act and concealing a warped intelligence.

Garran seemed the better possibility. He'd made and broken sheriffs, prosecutors, and judges. He'd been intimately involved with the county for a long time. He was ring-smart and ruthless, and he had a continuing desire for power I'd witnessed personally. Maybe power hadn't, for some unknown reason, been enough.

On the other hand, maybe I was seeing something because I was looking for it. I had no real answers—yet.

At four o'clock I went back to my office. I had a visitor.

He was sitting on my lumpy couch with his hat tilted down over his eyes. He wore a rumpled summer cord suit. A battered briefcase sat beside him.

He looked up at me with a quizzical grin splitting his black face. "Janitor let me in," he said. "Didn't like it, but finally did when I told him I was a business associate of yours on a case which has attracted attention afar and in many quarters." He grinned wider. "I had a notion to tell him I was your first cousin. He didn't appear to be a close-mouthed man. That would have finished your hash in this town, if it isn't finished already."

"Hello, Nero," I said, and grinned back.

He got to his feet easily, like a great cat, and we shook hands. My hands are big, but he hid my right one in his right one, mangled it gently, and then let it go.

I sat down behind my desk and he took the chair on the other side. I dug in my drawer and came up with the bottle of Beam and a couple of glasses and poured. He took his and drank it down.

"Haven't seen you since law school," he said. "I heard you moved down here awhile back." He set the glass down gently. I poured him another. "I also heard why. I'm sorry, Sam."

I nodded. "It's good to see you, Tiger," I said.

His eyes got a little softer remembering the nickname.

"I'm working for the United International Movement. You listen to the right-wingers and we're a bunch of commies. You listen to the left-wingers and we don't go near far enough. My people let me come down to see if you needed any help."

"I've never tried a murder case," I admitted.

"It's like anything else," he said, still smiling. "The only thing you have to remember is that some poor bastard's life is involved." He sipped at the drink. "Pretty good whiskey," he said. "Tell me about the case."

I looked him over. We'd been close friends in law school, but I'd lost track of him after we graduated, lost track of all of them when disaster came. He had a huge, finely made ebony body and had been on a couple of All-American teams his senior year in undergraduate school. Knee problems had ended hopes of a pro career, so he'd gone to law school. I'd found there that his brain was better than his body. It ticked and clicked and computed and split hairs and then went dead to the point. I used to play Casino with him, but it was like trying to beat God. You could win a game if you were lucky enough, but not through skill. He could wait until the last cards were dealt and then tell you what four you held and what suits they were in. He was a big black man who saw the world for what it was, swallowed the salt, and grinned back. There was no one I could think of I'd rather have on my side. His full name was Nero Arnold Crabtree and he'd been Order of the Coif, editor of the law review, and summa cum laude in law school.

I told him most of what I knew and had found, leaving out Tarman's treatment of Al, leaving out Jan.

When I was done, he said, "Then you think he's innocent?"

I nodded. "I hope."

"You want some help?"

"You betchem. I'm not proud."

"You'll get it," he said. "I'll stick around for a few days, go with you to talk to some of the local black people. Maybe I can get something out of Mrs. Calling or Jefferson Jones you haven't managed. Then we'll kick it around. You'll have to do most of the work. I've got to go back and forth between here, the capital, and Washington. I've got things on the fire. But I'll block out time and be here to help with the trial." He looked over at me. "They let me do pretty much what I want to do, the organization does. I'd just as soon help a friend."

"OK," I said. "Where are you staying?"

"I haven't found out yet."

"You can stay with me."

"No," he said with finality. "There are people in town who'll look after me. I appreciate the offer, but my staying with you could hurt both of us and the case. Black people don't trust a black man with honkey-type friends. I'm supposed to call a Mrs. Garran. She's a honkey, too, but she's accepted and used. Is she related to the guy you were listing as one of your possible suspects?"

"Only his wife."

He grinned. "Then I'll check in with her and go where she sends me and snoop some tonight. I'll see you here at your office in the morning at about nine."

I nodded. We went out into the hall together and the janitor watched us suspiciously.

He got into his car and we waved good-bye. When he'd vanished I went on down to the City Club and had a couple of martinis on the rocks diluted by scathing looks from some of the other patrons.

I felt like a fair maiden must in a horse opera when John Wayne came over the hill just as the villain was about to do unspeakable things to her. Nero did that for me. The responsibility was still mine, but now I had someone to share it with.

I remembered when I was in law school and behind because of holding outside jobs to make ends meet. Come finals time, Nero had the stuff and Nero would spend the time needed to knock what I needed to know into my thick skull—enough to keep me in and off probation. That was when I'd had a wife and child. Not so long ago in one way, but another time and place, something I no longer wanted to remember clearly.

8

I HAD A date to meet Jan at eight o'clock, so I ate a sandwich at the City Club, then went to my apartment and washed up. I sat around and read the newspaper until it was time to go. There was nothing new in it about Jones—or me—except that the grand jury had indicted him for murder.

It was almost dark when I went out of my apartment and drove to Jan's. She lived in town with another girl who worked for the telephone company.

Jan was dressed in something sleek and black, and she looked almost fragile in the dim light of her hallway.

I'd thought of asking her about the stories in yesterday's paper, but decided against it. She didn't write the snide editorials, and the news stories had undoubtedly been written by McGill. It might start the evening off wrong. And it was an evening I wanted very much to be right.

We drove to the Oasis and drank tall Scotch-and-waters. We danced to the soft music of the jukebox. She danced well. She had the kind of body that was made for dancing, with a sort of proud softness to it. I itched to close my arms around her tightly. Instead, we danced, if not sedately, at least decently for the times. You get to do your own thing these days on the dance floor, but it's permissible to do those things with others, even those of the opposite sex.

In between dances we talked. I didn't tell her about Nero. The paper would find out about him soon enough and she'd be duty-bound, if told now, to report it to McGill. There was no need for that to happen until it had to. We talked instead about her family. She had five brothers and two sisters. Two of her brothers had been in Nam when I was there. Her parents were living and had a large farm upstate.

"At least I grew up well fed," she said, laughing.

"I can see that for myself," I said appraisingly. I looked at her tan arms and fine, fine body.

"Don't look at me like that," she said softly. "It gives me the shivers. I keep thinking you're about to bite me."

"It's a thought."

She drew away, but only a little. "How about your family?" she asked.

"Haven't much left. My mother and father both died while I was in Vietnam. I've got an older brother who lives in Detroit. He writes when he needs money. That's all there is."

Her hand touched mine and her voice was tentative. "You said you'd been married?"

"Yes."

"Divorced?"

"No. My wife and son died in an auto accident about a year after I graduated from law school."

"I'm sorry. I don't think you want to talk about it."

"It's all right," I said, but it really wasn't. "We had an old clunker and the tires weren't much good. She was driving down to see her mother—her dad died when she was a kid—and she was driving fast. She loved to do that. She took great joy in life. One of the tires blew and that was all there was for both of them." I picked up my glass and took a pull on my drink. My hand was steady—not like it had once been.

"I tried to stay there where I was, but I couldn't. So one day I picked up and came down here." I nodded. "It's better here."

"You loved her very much," she said. It was a statement.

"Yes, I did. We got married in our last year of undergraduate school. We didn't have a dime, but she could take the good things and the bad and make them all come out like laughter." I looked up at Jan. "She could make me laugh. It's something I wish I had in me, that gift of laughter."

"Thank you for telling me," she said. "About her, I mean." She watched me with eyes that were both wise and warm. "Now I know a bit more about what makes Sammy run and why he ran down here."

I felt a small irritation and it must have shown in my eyes.

She didn't say anything for a while and neither did I. Then the music started again as someone fed the juke. We got up to dance and the bad moment passed.

Her eyes watched me while we danced and I tried to fathom what I saw in them. When the music stopped we stood for a moment watching each other.

"Let's get out of here," I said. "I need to talk to Doc Mahoney, and we might as well drink his whiskey and listen to his tapes if he's home."

She nodded.

Doc Mahoney lived in a new ranch-style monstrosity on the highway near town. Once, when he'd suggested I move in with him; I'd considered the offer and decided against it. We heard different drums and Doc's beat wasn't even close to mine. Seeing each other occasionally, we were close. If we'd been living together, I doubted it would remain that way. You get to know a person too well and allowances you make when you're merely good friends don't hold up.

You could tell he was home from two hundred yards away. He liked light, lots of light. His black Eldorado was in the driveway and the windows were open in the house. When we parked behind his car I could hear the sound of music. Diamond.

I banged on the door until he let us in. If he'd been drinking it didn't show, but then it seldom did.

He slid the door back and blinked into the darkness. "Ah," he said. "Friend April, with a maiden in need of rescue. Come in, come right in."

I grinned and followed him in with Jan on my arm.

Jan busied herself at the tape player in the living room. Doc and I went on out to the bar in what had once been a dining room. Now it was a library-bar, but mostly bar.

"Some fine lady," Doc said, nodding out the door to where Jan was. "I can see you've absorbed the lessons I taught you at my knee. But beware the master. She'd probably prefer a doctor like myself to a scarred-up lawyer."

"You're such a joy to me," I said. "I'm glad I didn't appear on your doorstep in need of urgent medication, because I haven't much faith in your ability to diagnose when one of the opposite sex is around."

He competently mixed Scotch with water and handed me two. "This is what I prescribe for both of you."

"Stay in here a moment," I said. "I want to talk to you about some things before we go back into the living room and you try to backdoor me."

He smiled. "Business before pleasure."

I took Jan a drink and then returned.

"She's much too good for you," Doc said when I returned to the bar. "I saw your picture in the paper yesterday and looked for you last night to compliment you on an excellent likeness. Sam April, vampire."

I grinned.

"Furthermore," he continued, "I want you to know I'll send a fifty-buck bouquet should you turn out to be right and get too close to the killer and become victim number two. Or if it turns out the Klan still is around."

89

I asked lightly, "Would you miss me, Doc?"

His voice became almost serious. "You, Sam, are crafted completely of wool and are several yards wide. You're truly blue. You're the kind of guy who wins the Parcheesi game for Harvard in the last sixteenth of a second. I, on the other hand, am shoddy goods and my color, instead of blue, runs from a shocking pink about the eyeballs to a livid green in my infected urinary system." He was still for a second. "You fill a need in me."

"Enough of this lovemaking," I said. "This isn't my week for boys. I need to ask you serious questions."

He took a long sip of his drink. "What do you want to know?"

"Are you positive Julia Cunnel was raped?"

He frowned a little. "Most of the signs of rape were present. There was internal and external bruising. Her clothes and underclothes were ripped and torn, but my test for semen was negative. My medical opinion, at trial, will be she was raped."

I leaned against the bar. "Was there anything unusual about it I don't know about?"

He thought for a moment. "I guess maybe there was," he said slowly. "I won't say exactly strange; maybe different's a better word. I interned in a big city and I made maybe a thousand ambulance runs. I saw cases of rape and attempted rape. They usually follow a pattern—rape and run—unless the person committing the crime is too rough or he kills to conceal. The woman can die if she fights too hard while the rape is being perpetrated, or she may die afterward of a combination of shock and injuries. Sometimes a rapist even kills when the act is completed because that's a part of what he desires or he doesn't want a live witness. Julia Cunnel, however, was dead or almost dead before the rape was attempted. By that I mean she was struck several blows with the hatchet, dying within moments from those blows, and then raped."

"How do you know that?"

He ran a hand through his thick hair. "There was nothing under her fingernails and they were long ones. If she was conscious when raped, she'd probably have clawed her attacker. My medical opinion is that whoever raped her did it after she was dead."

"But you said her clothes and underclothes were torn?"

He smiled. "Maybe your murderer, assuming for the moment it was someone other than Jones, was just as eager whether she was dead or not."

I thought about that. "Then whoever did it slipped up on her, smashed her a couple of times with a hatchet, then tore her clothes, then raped her, and then ran?"

"Kee-rect," he said. "And he raped her while she was dying or there wouldn't have been any bruising."

"And you say you've heard of it happening that way before?"

He waved a hand through the air. "Sure. It's not usual, but it happens. One happened that way when I was interning, but it was on the other shift and I didn't see it. I just heard about it when I came on duty, got the gory details. Necrophilia in all its glory."

I thought about that. It didn't mean anything to me, except to confirm my own theory that murder and not rape was the prime objective of Julia Cunnel's attacker.

"How about Sanders, the lawyer, Doc?" I asked. "Did you get called on that one?"

He nodded. "That was one of the strangest ones I've seen down here. People having coronaries do funny things, but I never saw one that shot a gun through his own window while he was having a fatal." His eyes met mine. "You think there's some connection between Sanders's death and Julia Cunnel's?"

"That depends on whether or not he was murdered. Could he have been?"

He shook his head. "I don't think so. It looked like another heart attack to me, but like most times, I didn't have a lot of hours to spend on it. Too many sick people around to worry about the dead ones."

"Did you treat Sanders?"

He snorted. "Every doctor in town treated him at one time or another. He was a chronic. Every time he had a pain he changed doctors. He was an old man with a bad heart. Every day that heart got older. He wanted a cure. He'd had open-heart five years before he died. He did all right for a time after that, but you can't cure age."

I nodded.

"He was a tight old bastard. He'd call me at the office for advice or drop by the house at night rather than pay for an office call. He owed me money when he died, but I never sent a bill. Should have, I guess, because he reportedly died loaded."

"Who got it?" I asked.

He looked up at me. "Way I heard it, Paul Garran's wife got it. She was his niece and closest living relative, and they didn't find a will."

I felt excitement rise within me. "You mean no will was ever probated for a lawyer like Sanders? That's not normal. Half his practice was probate work."

"They sure never found one," he said vaguely, looking toward the living room, where Jan was.

"Look, Doc," I said when his eyes finally came back, "be honest with me. Tell me the truth. If a death looks to you like a normal death, do you ever check it further?"

He shrugged. "I don't claim to be foolproof and I know damned well the sheriff and the police aren't, either. The problem is we don't have enough doctors in this town and I'm usually too busy to look at more than the bare face of things. I can't go around digging on hunches. The police aren't that much. They haven't got the training." He looked at me. "I suppose Sanders's death could have been, on an outside chance, murder. I don't believe it was, but it could have been."

I nodded. "Thanks for the admission, Doc. Any suspects for me?"

He took me seriously. "Sure, I've got one. You'd need someone who's smart and ruthless and knows the town. And any killer would have to be a little nuts, especially the multiple killer you're suggesting. I still think you're baying at the moon for lack of something better to do. But I'll tell you something I know which I didn't learn as a result of my medical practice. Your friend Paul Garran spent a year in an asylum a long time ago and I heard he was damned near broke when Sanders died. I'll tell you something else I've heard. I've heard his wife spends too much time down at Jefferson Jones's house and in the black neighborhood to suit Garran. I've also heard she's been seen going in and out of your client's house."

Excitement quickened. "What was Garran supposedly suffering from when he was in the asylum?"

He shook his head. "I don't know. He's never been my patient, and what I told you is barroom hearsay."

"He could have kept a key to the shed," I said softly, trying it on for size. "Maybe Julia Cunnel knew about the will and what happened to it. By killing Julia he could revenge himself on Al for maybe fooling with his wife, if he was, and get rid of someone who may have happened on a copy of the will and maybe have been looking for some pay for it."

"You're adventuring in fantasy again," Doc said.

"I've found a new road to explore is all." I nodded at him. "How about Mrs. Calling, Doc?"

He shrugged again. "She's dead. I give her four or five months, but don't quote me. She's loaded with cancer. She's had radiation, chemotherapy, and I did an exploratory on her a couple of months ago and had to sew her back up. I told her if she got to one of the big clinics maybe she'd have a chance with interferon, but she really doesn't have one. She wants me to operate on her, but it's too late. It was too late a long time ago. But all she's got is hope and I try to keep that up. We talk brave together."

I nodded. "I figured as much when I saw her." I was silent until his eyes came up to mine. "How about you, Doc? Did you know Julia Cunnel?"

He passed over it lightly. "What girl don't I know? I try to pass myself around, give them all a few moments' pleasure."

"True," I said. "You dated her, then?"

He nodded. "Several times. She quickly became too pallid for my tastes."

"You might make me a good suspect, Doc. You're down around that neighborhood where she died all the time. You dated Julia Cunnel—"

He cut me off. "I never kill them when I'm done with them, Sam. I save them for a rainy day."

"Trouble is I can't find a good motive for you. Maybe she watered your whiskey or stole your tapes?"

He smiled. "On that we'll rejoin the lady."

I nodded abstractedly.

He took my empty glass. "I'll fix another drink first."

He busied himself with ice and water, and Jan, hearing the sound of ice against glass, came out for a refill.

"The good doctor was just telling me," I said, for her benefit, "that he's got an absolute preventive for pregnancy."

Mahoney grinned hugely. "He means abstinence. I don't recommend it."

Jan colored nicely. "You needn't worry about that with this one," she said softly, nodding at me. "I'm not sure he's interested in girls."

"Well, I am," Doc said hastily. "Let's leave him here.

I've got a revolver and he can play Russian roulette to amuse himself while you and I go out and watercolor the town." He turned to me. "I'll put five bullets in instead of one."

I sighed. "At least it'll be a short game."

He handed us more drinks and turned up the tape player in the large living room. There was an imitation fire in the fireplace—one of those electric things—and Jan and I danced to its summer-incongruous flickering light. Around the room there were shelves of bright-jacketed books. Doc read science fiction in addition to his medical texts, so lurid covers of spaceships and bug-eyed monsters looked back at us. It was a bachelor's room. There was dust on the books, and the rugs showed patches of discoloration no wife would ever have been able to stand.

"I like your friend," Jan said, mouth close to my ear.

"Not too much, I hope."

Her teeth nibbled reassuringly at my ear. They were sharp, little teeth, but I didn't mind.

We danced. In a while I quit thinking about what Doc had told me and thought only of her.

The ringing of the telephone brought me back to reality. Doc answered it and talked in low tones for a moment or two. He went into the other room and got his black bag.

"That was the hospital. I've got to go there now," he said. He looked us over thoughtfully. "Why don't you stick around. I won't be long, and we can do away with the rest of the Scotch when I get back. Doc Kelly's supposed to be taking my calls tonight, but I've got a chronic at the hospital who insists on seeing me." He smiled. "I should be back in an hour or so."

I looked at Jan and she looked at me. I could read nothing in her eyes. "We'd better go," I said. "It's getting late."

"Stick around. You don't have to go," Doc said.

Jan gave a little nod of the head. "We'll stay," she said. She turned away from us, went to the tape player, and put another tape in.

Doc winked at me and went out his door. In a moment I heard the sound of his car engine as it receded down the drive.

Jan turned from the tape player and came into my arms, pressing warmly at me with her fine body. I could feel, and soon see, that it was a very good body. She looked at me from the couch where we'd fallen and her eyes were pools of soft, blue river. I dived in. The water was warm and deep.

She spoke so softly that I almost lost her voice. "I'm competing with a ghost for you, Sam. A ghost has lots of advantages, because the bad things are forgotten but the good things aren't." Her eyes were now a million years old. "But I have some advantages."

I kissed her and stopped the words for a moment.

She said, "He expects us to do something—men always do—and there isn't much time." She kissed me more urgently.

There was time enough.

9

IN THE MORNING I awoke when the sun walked in the window. I tasted the burned flavor of retreaded Scotch. I got up and took a lengthy shower with the water hot and then cold, and I drank V-8 juice in large amounts and coffee in larger. In a while I was almost human.

It had developed into quite a party after Doc returned. He'd brought a cute little nurse with him. I remembered some of the early parts of it, but not much of the later. I did remember that I'd had Jan drive home.

My car was parked in front. Someone had very carefully lined the backsplash pan, between bumper and trunk, with empty Scotch bottles and beer cans. That should be a joy to the local police. I removed the debris and carried it back to the garbage.

Nero was holding up the door to my office. He smiled knowingly when he saw me. I opened the door and we went in. My mail from the day before had been poked through the mail opening and was scattered on the floor. I picked it up while Nero slid his bulk into a seat.

Besides the inevitable bills and circulars, there were four anonymous letters. They were pretty much the same. I read them and then handed them on to Nero. In the letters I was a dirty name or an obstructor of justice and Al was a vicious killer. Two of the writers made it plain they'd never cross the doorstep of my office, a third stated that if I ever got within range he'd shoot me on sight. The fourth was the most interesting. It was evident that the writer was not heterosexual. He had an interesting fate in store for me.

Nero smiled when he read that one. "You'd better watch yourself in public rest rooms," he said. He yawned. "I was up late, but from the look of you I've more natural resistance to the fruit of the grape than you. I talked to your girlfriend, Mrs. Garran, and she put me up for the night in her house. Her husband is presently out of town, so we drank some of his whiskey and some influential blacks were invited in. It appears that there's some doubt in their collective minds as to Al's innocence. I told them you were satisfied. Some of them may help us; others won't." He smiled laconically. "After retiring, I was awakened about three by Mrs. Garran. I had to fight hard to save my virginity."

I nodded. "I'd heard that. I hope you were successful."

"My hymen is safe. I have it at home preserved in an old mason jar."

I smiled.

He said, "Enough of the trials and tribulations of po' ole Nero Crabtree. You've been busting to lay something on me ever since we came in. Tell all."

So I told him about Sanders, the lack of a will, Paul Garran and his possible asylum stay, and the rest Doc had passed on the night before. He sat there and listened intently, a black statue of the Thinker. And in his eyes I could see a bit of the excitement that I felt.

"You want to see Garran today?" he asked. "He's supposed to be back."

I thought on it. "No, not today. I want to see him sometime. Let's go see some of your black people. If I can place Garran near where Julia Cunnel was killed or even just tie him to her, then that would be something concrete. I'd like a lot of ammunition before I try to tangle with Paul Garran. He's big poison locally."

"Okay," he said. "Let's haul."

"First, to the jail. You need to meet our client. Besides, I sent a motion for a change of judge over and I want to pick it up from him."

"Why are you changing judges?" he asked.

"Mostly because the bastards in town don't want me to."

"That's a good enough reason."

We went out into the bright sunlight.

We picked up the signed motion from a sheriff's deputy and then went in to see Al. I introduced Nero to him. I thought it made Al feel better just looking at Nero.

"You mean you're going to help Mr. April here represent me?" he asked.

Nero nodded.

Al looked at the size of him. "I'd hate to be on the jury that tries to convict me."

I looked at Nero and saw he was thinking what I was. "We might not use a jury. We may just use a judge from away from here."

Al smiled. I could do no wrong. "Whatever you guys decide." His eyes were full of life.

Nero said, "You sit tight in here. For God's sake, don't you mess up. If you can be got out of this thing, we'll get you out." He looked down at Al and radiated a confidence I wished I could share.

When Al returned inside the cell block, the old white-haired man was sitting at the table. He looked up at us with complete boredom. There was a pencil in front of him, but the broom still lay on the floor where last I'd seen it. There was some interesting new art along the walls. Women with prominent physical features. It appeared the old man had found a new hobby.

We took the motion up to the clerk's office, file-marked it, and used one of the envelopes there to mail a copy to Rhinehoff.

In the afternoon Nero and I called on some of the black population of the town. We didn't learn much. Jefferson Jones, Al's brother, didn't remember any more than he'd first told me. Mrs. Calling, her wasted body rocking slowly in her chair, repeated her same story—more firmly this time. We checked the rest of the houses in the near neighborhood of Al's house on the possibility that someone might have seen a car or a person entering the graveyard, but there was nothing. Most of the neighborhood had been asleep. Those who remembered being awake remembered nothing out of the ordinary.

At five-thirty, hot, frustrated, and perspiring, we went to my apartment for a beer and a shower and then sat around my tiny front room and talked.

"The big question now becomes," Nero said, "when do we play tag with Paul Garran?"

"Soon," I said. "I feel like this will business is the crux of the whole situation. I'd like to talk to Julia Cunnel's people. Maybe they'll know something." I looked at him. "What's on your agenda for tonight?"

"You and I are attending a party. A very elite sort of party. The local chapter of the United International Movement is giving it for us. It's out at Mrs. Garran's and I'm under orders to get you there, too.

"I got a date," I said.

"Fine. Bring her along."

"She works for the newspaper."

That slowed him, but he nodded.

I called Jan and it was OK with her. In fact, she was intrigued.

So at seven-thirty we went to a party.

The Garran house was out in the country, about ten miles from town. It sat up on a bluff and overlooked the river. It was a big, rich house. There was a tree-shaded lane that led up to it. The road was well kept and heavily hedged. The house was long and rambling with lots of glass and a lighted swimming pool behind it. It was a house that had cost money to build and more money to maintain.

Jan held tight to my hand when we went through the door. Her face was subdued and watchful. Mrs. Garran opened the door for us and I saw again that rigid, determined jaw. She held out her hand and I shook it. Then Nero shook it.

"I'm glad to see you again, Mr. April." She eyed Jan with both distrust and disapproval. "You work for the newspaper, don't you?"

Jan smiled. "I'm not working tonight."

Mrs. Garran's face didn't change. "Of course not, dear. Come in and meet the rest of our guests."

She took Nero possessively by the arm, and Jan and I followed behind. We went into the living room. It was crowded with people. There were black people and white people. They drank and talked in small groups all around the room. By double doors a bar had been set up. One of the waiters from the City Club was busily tending it. People I knew nodded at me. I got drinks for Jan and myself at the bar and we wandered into the crowd.

Jefferson Jones sat uncomfortably on the edge of a white couch in the middle of the room, listening to what was going on around him, his soft hands moving nervously, his smile fixed and unwavering. Nero had drifted away somewhere and Jan was talking to Mrs. Gilligan, whose husband ran one of the local clothing stores. I went over to talk to Jefferson.

"Hello, Mr. April," he said, getting up.

"Hello, Mr. Jones," I said. We shook hands formally. I tried to think of something to say. "Good party?" I finally asked.

He looked me over. He was carrying a heavy load. "Yeah," he said. "Good party." He put a hand on my shoulder. A little of his drink slopped out on the rug.

"Goddamn bunch of hypocrites," he said. "They don't give a damn about Al. They'd like to see him cook. Then they could write things and form more committees about it; they could have a vigil outside the prison when they finally get around to frying Al. They could pray."

"It's better than it used to be," I said.

He looked at me and carded me in with the others in the room. "That's sure right," he said heartily. He nodded and wandered away to get another drink, and I had that curious feeling you get sometimes of having lost something, but not knowing exactly what was lost. I stood there in the middle of the room, feeling flat. I didn't even feel much like having another drink. Then I saw Mrs. Garran beckoning to me.

"Come into the study, young man," she said. "I want a chance to talk to you privately."

I followed her. The study was a place full of shining furniture and shelves of carefully dusted modern novels in bright jackets, leaning correctly, like guests for a weekend not certain of their welcome. She motioned me into a chair that was unsure of my weight and she turned on all the lights so that no one who came upon us would make the mistake that more than conversation was our interest.

I was happy she did. Like Nero, I have some pride.

I studied her. The harsh light was bad for her. I could see lines in her face beneath heavy makeup. Sooner or later I was going to have to accuse her husband of murder. I wondered how she'd take it. Knowing some of her interests and suspecting others, I wondered if it would touch her at all.

"I'm much interested in this case," she said. "Alphonse, of course, worked for my husband. . . ."

"Where's your husband tonight, Mrs. Garran?" I asked respectfully.

She pursed her lips. "He doesn't hold with this, so I

sent him off to a meeting of his own in town. He believes what he wants to believe, and I believe what I want to. We're happy that way."

"I see. Might I ask you if you know his whereabouts on the night Julia Cunnel died?"

Her eyes were only slightly curious. "Why would you want to know that?"

"I'm checking the whereabouts of everyone who had any connection with Alphonse Jones."

She nodded slowly. "I see. I'm not really sure where he was. I was home that night, but I believe he was out."

"Did you or your husband know Julia Cunnel?"

"Mr. April, this is a small town. And Julie worked for my great-uncle in his law office. Such a lovely child. A shame to die so young." She transfixed me with her eyes. "You're asking all the questions. Now I'd like to ask one. What are Alphonse's chances?"

"Improving," I said blandly. "The prosecution has a strong, but circumstantial, case. Nero and I have found some things which may help Al."

"Such as?"

"I'm not at liberty to disclose them, Mrs. Garran." I smiled at her. "Whenever I am at liberty, you can be assured you'll be the first to know."

She wasn't satisfied. "If I'm to help, then I'll have to have something to tell the others to convince them."

I hesitated and then said, "The only thing I can tell you is that we're trying to find a motive for Julia Cunnel's death. When we find that, we'll have something to run with."

She shook her head. "Well, that's not much for me to go on."

"It's all I can do for now." I decided to press on with her. "You were talking about Mr. Sanders. I checked yesterday and noted he'd died intestate."

She nodded. "I can tell you a little about that. I believe

Paul told me once that my great-uncle had made a will after he and Paul fell out where I wasn't a beneficiary. When they reconciled, he destroyed that will and apparently didn't have a chance to draw up another before his untimely death." She shrugged. "Paul takes care of the business and that sort of thing. I just run the house."

I looked around me and got up gingerly from the fragile chair. "And a lovely house it is."

"I'm quite proud of it," she said. "I grew up without a lot of money and always wanted a big house. Now I have it." She got up also. "We should rejoin the party. Mr. Crabtree promised to say a few words."

We walked together back into the living room.

Garran could have put on a sham reconciliation with Sanders. Julia Cunnel would have known of Sanders's real feelings or perhaps a new will, so she'd also have to die. But why the time lag? At least I knew Garran hadn't been home the night of the killing. He was clever and ruthless. I hoped I'd find something that made him not clever enough.

Nero was already speaking. The lights in the living room had been turned down and the bar was vacant. Nero had his back to the piano. I found Jan and took her hand.

Nero was talking in his easy manner about the rights of man. Translated, it was the "I have a dream" speech rewritten by Nero Crabtree. The only strong light in the room shone on his face. It was the kind of speech that most of the audience had come to hear, and they listened raptly. He finished up by saying that the work of the people in the room was felt and appreciated and needed.

It was pretty good, but once Nero's eyes flicked across mine and he lowered one eyelid just a ghost of a fraction, and that look reminded me of what I knew Nero really believed. Nero believed that each man was what he let the world make him into.

I remembered him in school. Sometimes, when the arguments about busing, pay, jobs, and the rest would wax hot, Nero would take the side of the antis. He'd say he really didn't give a damn about being accepted, because he was as smart or smarter than those people who decided to accept or not accept him. The only thing he really wanted was to be allowed to compete, and he thought he had that right and had had it for most of his lifetime. He said he'd fight to keep that right.

He stopped talking and there was a little ripple of applause. Someone turned the lights back on. They started serving drinks again at the bar. I got refills for Jan and myself. I noticed that Mrs. Garran served a very inferior brand of Scotch, but it was, at least, Scotch.

No one asked me to speak. I was glad.

Jan and I took our drinks and went out to the patio that overlooked the pool and the river.

"I was watching your face when Nero was talking," she said. "You two guys really like each other, don't you?"

"Yep."

"But this stuff he was preaching—this United International Movement, all men are brothers—doesn't touch you, does it?"

I tried to explain. "I don't care about whole peoples or their problems or complaints. Those things are beyond me. I care about individuals. If I like them, it's OK with me if they're black, white, yellow, or red, go to church on Saturdays, Sundays, or not at all."

She smiled and the full moon got hotter. "I like the way you walk, too. Like you're hunting something."

I nuzzled her a nuzzle. "I am."

She nuzzled back. "Are you completely tolerant?"

"Nah," I said. "I'm against women who don't drink. Drink up."

We stood for a time watching the moon.

"Did you know Julia, Jan?"

"Julia Cunnel?" She nodded. "I ran across her once or twice."

"You used to date Ken Cavin, didn't you?"

She turned to face me. "I had a couple of dates with him."

"He's very handsome," I said.

She nodded shortly. "Don't get my temper up, Sam. If you're looking for suspects close to you, it was I who dropped him. I got damned tired of him checking himself in every mirror we came to. I got tired of dull conversation and retreating all over the front seat of his pretty, pretty car to keep away from hands that were either combing his hair or trying to get in mine."

"Sure," I said, drawing her close. "Is he as stupid as he acts?"

She hesitated. "Not stupid. Just very arrogant and extremely conceited."

"Could he kill someone?"

She shook her head. "I'm not an expert. I do know he got wild when I quit dating him. He grabbed me on the street one night when I came out of the movies. He jerked me into his car. I had to fight." She grinned. "I used a shoe on him."

10

IT'S OFTEN SAID that lawyers drink too often and too much and that that drinking is one of the major failings of the profession. I must admit it's so. There are some lawyers who don't drink and others who drink in fine moderation, but many of those in the profession do drink copiously. I'm not one of the exceptions. Maybe, for me, it's the idea of worrying about someone else's troubles day after day. Certainly the work isn't back-breaking, although the hours can be long, especially in trials. But I get a release in alcohol. I can forget things I needn't remember when the office closes.

I stood in Doc Mahoney's bathroom, examining myself in the too-bright light of his mirror. Outside I could hear Doc and Nero going over the ethics of both the medical and the legal professions, their voices high and querulous. They'd fallen for each other like sophomores at a mixer. Love at first fight.

I supported myself partially with a hand against the wall and examined my face. Several nights of drinking had left my eyes red and bloodshot. I'd shaved imperfectly and under one cheek there was a growth of hair I'd mostly missed. I was drunk and knew it. I felt wasted.

In a while I went back out. Jan was playing tapes, volume down. Doc and Nero argued on. Doc's voice was heavy. Every once in a while his eyes would close for a long moment before he reentered the fray.

I stood in the middle of the room.

"Come on," I announced. "We're going."

Nero looked up at me. "Where are we going, Sam?"

"To the graveyard," I said.

"Not me," Doc said. "I get enough of graveyards. Nero here says that my bunch is populating them with our mistakes." He smiled and closed his eyes.

Jan eyed me doubtfully.

Nero smiled. "Lead on, oh fearless leader."

We drove to the graveyard, abandoning Doc on his couch. First we stopped at a drive-in and Nero forced black coffee down me until I was soberer. That took some time. When I did begin to straighten up, going to the graveyard didn't seem like quite the idea it had been at first. But it probably was no worse an idea than stopping at Doc's on the way back from Garran's. But we had stopped and I'd been gratified when Doc and Nero had taken to each other the way a pair of brilliant egotists sometimes will—quarrelsomely, but with mutual respect.

Mrs. Calling's house was dark when we passed it, but as I slowed, I fancied I could hear a creaking noise and supposed that was the sound of her rocking chair on the front porch.

Jan moved closer to me. The moon was down and it was dark.

"I don't like being here. It's too spooky for me."

"The ghouls won't bite on your tender flesh," I said. "I'll protect you, if you'll protect me."

"Who's going to protect me?" Nero asked plaintively.

"They won't be able to find you in the dark as easy as us," I said. "Just don't open your mouth. They'll see your teeth."

I stopped at Jones's house. "Now, if the police theory is correct, then the girl came along here on foot. She was on her way home from the movie and so she cut across the graveyard."

"She was braver than I'd be," Jan said, shivering.

"Me too," Nero echoed.

I ignored them. "Al Jones wakes up from his alcoholic sleep. He hears or sees the girl and follows her into the graveyard. There he kills and then rapes her."

Thoughts played stoop tag in my head. If Jones had come out of the house with an ax when Julia Cunnel walked past, wouldn't she have seen him? She'd have run or fought. So if Al was the killer, he couldn't have just followed her. He'd have had to lie in wait for her. That meant premeditation. I thought it would be easier for someone else to plan the crime than a man drunk on cheap wine.

The night was dark-dark around us. Even the starlight was blotted out by the trees that bordered the road into the graveyard.

I drove on in.

The first thing I saw was Doc's Cadillac. It was parked at the side of the access road. The left front door was open and a pair of feet hung out. The car was parked very close to the spot where I knew Julia Cunnel had been killed.

I stopped the car and no one said a word. We watched Doc's feet. I felt fear run through me. Then Doc raised his head from the right side of the car and blinked at the light of my headlights. Nero sighed beside me.

"Jesus," Jan said.

I opened my car door.

"Where's everyone been?" Doc asked amiably. "I decided to join the party. I've been waiting half an hour."

"I thought you'd bought it," I said softly.

Doc looked at me and finally comprehension came. He smiled. "I will go in bed, April—not like she went."

I left my car lights on and stepped to the far side of the road. There were tombstones on the other side, but none here yet. The vacant side was nearest Al's house. There was one huge tree near the road. A line of rose bushes, heavy with blood-red blooms, blocked easy entrance at one side of the tree and seemed even heavier on the other side. But my lights picked out an opening between roses and tree. I squeezed through it. Jan, Nero, and Doc squeezed through behind me. There was enough room to hide behind the bushes or the tree. When someone passed, a killer could have reached out from the opening and touched the passerby—or buried an ax.

Jan's hand sought mine. "Remind me to remind you that graveyards aren't my favorite date place. They give me the—"

I cut her off by kissing her. Nero and Doc explored around the tree. When I stopped kissing Jan, she leaned against me.

"Now I see your plan. You've returned to the scene of your crime and I'm the intended victim," she said softly against my ear. "Just like late-night television. Don't bother with the ax."

"Whoever did it almost had to hide behind here someplace. Now, let's walk up toward Al's house."

"Send Doc and Nero," she said, still hanging on. "You and I can stay here."

"We'll come back."

She shuddered bravely.

The four of us started out. There was a barely definable path. From it I could see a tiny light in Mrs. Calling's kitchen. The ground was summer-hard. The undergrowth became less dense as soon as we reached the wall that separated the graveyard from Al's property line. Nero, Doc, and I stepped over it and then I helped Jan. Her foot dragged over the old wall and a pebble fell.

I looked over at the wire fence that restrained Mrs. Calling's dogs. I saw no movement. I heard the small creaking sound I thought I'd heard before.

"Come on," I said urgently.

The dogs lay silently curled in their pen. I stopped at

the fence and yelled at them, but there was no movement. There was nothing near the pen to indicate what had happened to them, but I was almost certain they'd never move again.

The back door of Mrs. Calling's house was ajar. Doc beat me to it. He went in and the rest of us followed at his heels.

The creaking sound came from a rope. It was suspended over a beam that ran the length of the house. The dim light in the house came from one tiny bulb. There was only enough light to show where the creaking sound had emanated from. Mrs. Calling hung suspended from a rope, an overturned chair near her feet, her thin neck stretched and discolored, her eyes open. Whatever truth she'd withheld from me I'd never know now.

The hinged door to the dog run was bolted shut.

Doc looked at me. He was suddenly sober. "Get up on that chair and untie the rope. She may still be alive." He reached out and touched one of her hands. "No use."

He turned to Jan. "Go call the police. The telephone's in the bedroom."

She nodded, her face bloodless.

I righted the overturned chair and got on it. I'd seen death happen many times before, sometimes even to friends. But those deaths now seemed far away, the results of the gambling that men do with their lives in war.

I touched the end of the rope that encircled the beam. It was full of splinters.

Doc said, "Never mind, Sam. She's long gone. We'd better leave her until the police get here."

"Somebody killed her," I said.

Nero looked at me from where he stood by the window. "How do you know?"

"The rope's full of splinters. I think someone tied it around her neck, then pulled her up."

111

In a few moments I could hear sirens coming from far off. Doc and Nero and Jan and I went into the kitchen to wait for them. In the adjoining room the body still creaked against the rope and beam. I was certain I'd hear the sound in my dreams for the rest of my life.

I looked around the kitchen. It was clean as a spring rain, even though there wasn't much to it. There was a small refrigerator. There was an old wood stove, a plain wooden kitchen table, and four chairs. Everything was spotless. There was only one incongruity. There was a cup on the drain board that hadn't been washed and put away.

Whoever the killer was, he or she had come just as Mrs. Calling was finishing cleaning her kitchen.

Sleep was a long time arriving that night. It was late when the police finished their cursory examination of the house. They came up with one additional fact. In a wastebasket, wadded up, they found the beginning of a letter. It was addressed to me, but all it said was *Dear Mr. April.* Nothing else.

Tarman and the police dawdled. Doc told them that in his opinion the woman had been murdered. Nero watched all impassively from the background. After a while the police got tired of Nero and me, so they ran us out, but Doc stayed as coroner and Jan for the paper.

I went home and went to bed. When sleep finally came for me it brought dreams. There was a man with a large knife. Mrs. Calling and I were behind a tree, hiding. The trouble was, the tree was only two inches in diameter. First the masked killer would cut at one side of us and then at the other. I was protecting Mrs. Calling, but her eyes were dead and it wasn't any use. My chest hurt in the night and there was both pain and hate, but mostly there was fear. And someplace there was something I needed to remember but couldn't. The face of the being with the knife was hidden in fog and shadow and they were dropping hydrogen bombs again and I could see who/what was dropping them. All of them looked like wolves—big, hungry wolves.

Somehow the picture was missing focus. I woke up in the night and knew that. There were still things to be done. I wondered what the official reaction was going to be to the death of Mrs. Calling.

Garran had been out on the loose that night. As far as I knew, so had Tarman and Ken Cavin. Doc had gotten to the graveyard ahead of Jan, Nero, and me. The only suspect I could definitely rule out was Jan, and she'd never been a serious contender.

I found out early what the official reaction to Mrs. Calling was going to be. After I had my shave and shower and was ready for the world, I phoned Tarman at his office.

"Sam April, Ben," I said. "Did Doc come up with anything last night I don't know about?"

His voice sounded tired and I wondered if he'd made it into bed at all. "She probably died maybe twenty to thirty minutes before you got there. Her neck was crushed, and of course the rope strangled her, too."

"How about Al's case? Is this going to make a difference?"

"Why the hell should it?" He was silent for a moment. "I talked with the prosecutor about it. He feels the whole thing is a mere coincidence. There wasn't anything in Mrs. Calling's purse and it was open in her bedroom. The prosecutor thinks she maybe surprised someone going through her things."

"Any sign of anything else from the house being taken?"

"No."

"You know she knew more about Julia Cunnel than she was telling?"

"You say she did. I don't know it."

"How about the dogs? What killed them?"

"Poison. Probably strychnine. More probably cyanide. It doesn't mean much by itself."

"So that's where it lays?"

"That's it. Rhinehoff told me he was going to push for an early trial date on the girl's killing. As soon as you get a special judge."

"Tell Rhinehoff to call me. I'll agree on anyone that I'm sure the local powers can't get to."

"No kidding?"

"Sure."

11

REPORTERS AND HANGERS-ON were thick when Nero and I walked into the courthouse that morning. We brushed through them—noticed, but ignored for now. We went to the clerk's office and checked the records for commitments for insanity, but found none for Paul Garran. Nero didn't think this unusual. Many times such proceedings are voluntary and no record exists in any court unless the person under treatment attempts to terminate treatment while his doctors still want him to continue. Then, too, the commitment could have taken place in another county or even another state.

While we were there we checked the probate records for Sanders. Doc had been right about that. When no will was probated, Mrs. Garran had taken under the statutes governing intestacy. I whistled when I saw the final report. After taxes the amount she'd received was more than a million dollars.

Calla Simon was in her office and I took Nero in to meet her. She had her feet up on her desk with a fan blowing cool air on them. She took them down hastily.

"Good morning, madam," I said.

"Don't call me that. I've retired as a professional."

I smiled and introduced Nero.

"I heard some about you," she said, nodding, then turned back to me. "And I also heard we had another killing last night."

"We were on the scene."

"I also heard that. The word around here is that

there's no connection between the deaths of Julia Cunnel and Mrs. Calling despite the fact that they were done within a short distance of each other. The sheriff was giving the news people a break by passing out that word when I came in this morning. People on the street are starting to wonder out loud, not hard, but some. Rhinehoff was with the sheriff. He's been a busy bee."

I nodded. "Listen, Calla . . . we're looking for information. I told Nero that where the books leave off Calla Simon begins."

"Leave the butter off and ask away," she said.

"Paul Garran. Have you ever heard that he was committed to a mental institution?"

She pursed her lips. "Wherever did you get that?"

"Around."

"I never heard it, but I'll sure spread it now that I have. You might try the books in the capital."

"I'll check," Nero said.

Calla looked at us. "I'm glad you're here. Judge Weeks drove down as soon as Rhinehoff called him to qualify in the Jones case. He and Mart are in the judge's office now and I told him I'd try to find you."

"My, my," Nero said.

"That's sure fast service. I only agreed to him about an hour ago."

"That's the kind of service you get in a murder case."

"Before we go over there, can I use your typewriter or will you type something for me?"

"You'd better let me type it. I've seen you try to work one of these things."

I dictated her a motion to dismiss based on the fact that after giving oral notice I'd not been notified and had a chance to appear or have the defendant appear at the grand-jury hearing.

Rhinehoff was waiting in the judge's anteroom when Nero and I got there fifteen minutes later. I introduced

Nero, and Rhinehoff acknowledged him with a curt nod. Nero smiled. Rhinehoff went to the window and stood there looking out until the judge called us in.

Judge Robert Weeks was an aging man. He had thick white hair and eyebrows and a medium-large body. I'd had a case or two in front of him and liked him, so I'd readily agreed to him. He was a hard-nosed old trial man who'd practiced a lot of law before he was elected judge of the next circuit north. He'd taken over Judge Cleaves's office and was sitting behind the big desk smoking a black cigar and blowing heavy smoke rings.

His voice was harsh. "You gentlemen picked me as judge and the prosecutor seemed to think there was some urgency for me to get here, so I came. I've just now signed an entry qualifying." He looked us over curiously. "I think, at one time or another, I've met all you gentlemen."

Nero nodded.

"Is there anything special anyone wants to say this morning?" Weeks asked.

"I'd ask the court to enter an appearance for me for the defendant," Nero said.

Rhinehoff bristled. "I thought the defendant didn't have the money to hire counsel?"

"Mr. Crabtree isn't being paid by the defendant," I said. "He works for the United International Movement, which is interested in this case."

Rhinehoff sneered. "United International Movement . . ." He looked hard at Nero.

Nero looked back straight-faced. He affected his best drawl. "I wouldn't cause you no problems, Mr. Prosecutor." He grinned a little.

Rhinehoff reddened. "I get on very well with the local blacks. I don't intend to be insulted by some big butter-and-egg lawyer out of the capital in here to cause local problems. So don't insult me, Mr. Crabtree."

"Don't be insulting yourself," I said to him coldly.

Judge Weeks made an irritated little noise. He looked at Nero. "I've had you before in court, Mr. Crabtree. You're welcome any time in front of me. I'll have the docket sheet reflect your appearance."

Rhinehoff got to his feet. "I'd like to ask that this case be set for trial at the earliest possible date."

"Unseemly haste," I said.

Judge Weeks looked at me. "Do you have any objection to this case being set in the near future?"

"Not if we get complete cooperation on discovery, Your Honor. However, there's one additional matter." I reached into my pocket and got out the motion to dismiss I'd had Calla prepare. "I'd like to show this filed and serve one of the copies on Mr. Rhinehoff personally in your presence."

Rhinehoff took the pleading and read it without expression.

"This is rather ridiculous, Your Honor."

Judge Weeks looked us over. "Do you gentlemen want to argue it now and get it out of the way?" He nodded. "If not, I'll set a date for argument."

I smiled obligingly. "It's not Mr. Crabtree's or my intention to seek unneeded delays in this matter. After all, our innocent client is in jail and must remain there until trial. If Mr. Rhinehoff wants to argue this matter today, we'll oblige him."

Rhinehoff hastily got to his feet. "If the court will give me one moment, I'll look up the rule. Then we can proceed. It's my contention that this is merely an attempt at delay and has no legal standing. These two 'gentlemen' are trying to flimflam the court."

Judge Weeks raised a hand. "Please save your arguments. Look up what you need. The court will listen then."

Rhinehoff went out quickly, shutting the door hard

behind him. I think the look on my face worried him. Maybe he was seeing newspaper headlines.

Judge Weeks turned to us and smiled. He asked Nero about a case they'd both been in that had gone on to the appellate court. We talked about the weather, the condition of the court docket, how things were going in his circuit.

In a few moments Rhinehoff was back. I already knew my case citations by heart, or almost so, but I got out an advance sheet and a volume or two of the reporter system.

Arguments on motions don't normally receive much publicity, although in this case this motion might.

Rhinehoff argued the rule that stated baldly it was necessary to give written notice of a demand to question the grand jurors concerning prejudice toward a particular defendant, or to have that defendant appear in front of them to testify.

When he was done I cited the cases that made an exception to the rule when the death penalty was a part of the information. I could see Rhinehoff's face as I argued briefly. It kept getting longer and longer.

Rhinehoff waived rebuttal argument but said he'd like to research the matter further and call his prosecutor's council in the capital.

Judge Weeks got up from the desk and went to the window. For a long moment he was silent, looking out into the street. Then he turned back to us.

"The court feels no necessity to delay ruling."

Rhinehoff started to protest, but Weeks raised his hand. "It might interest you to know, Mr. Rhinehoff, that I took the first of the cases to the Supreme Court where this exception was granted. I've read the cases since and there's been no change. If it was changed, I'd try to change it again. A defendant who can die as a result of a prosecutor's whim not to inform his attorney of what's happening, after notice formal or informal, has whatever rights he claims at this stage of the proceeding." He nodded. "Start over."

"All right," Rhinehoff snarled. "We'll take the matter back to the grand jury."

"Will you agree to allow Judge Weeks to continue jurisdiction?" I asked.

He hesitated and then nodded.

Judge Weeks nodded and penciled something in his book. "All right. Mr. April, will you prepare an entry for the day?"

"Yes, sir."

He nodded and looked back down at his book, indicating by his silence that we were dismissed.

Nero and I followed Rhinehoff into the corridor. There he turned on us. I could see he was still white-hot. "You did that for one reason and one reason only, you and your buddy here. To get me bad publicity. You know the grand jury was fair and returned the only indictment they could have returned."

I shook my head. "Maybe, but I don't owe you a thing, Rhinehoff. You've been biting around on me in the local paper, trying to push yourself into whatever you figure is the next step up for you. That's your business. It's mine when you do it on my back and my client's back. It's also my business when you do it because it's politically motivated and you're told—'ordered' is a better word—to do it. I hear you're also one of the know-nothings giving out stories to the newspapers that there can be no connection between the killing of Julia Cunnel and Mrs. Calling's murder. Better look further, because it's going to get into the Jones trial. You thought you'd put one over with the grand jury, but you stung yourself. This time you'd better make sure it's not the same with the two murders."

His face became almost worried. "If you've got information, then give it to me or the police."

"I found the police dogging my trail the other night. I'll give them nothing. If I have information, it's because I went out and hunted for it. You'd better tell your ill-trained hot cops to do the same. And where I find something by looking for it, it becomes work product and isn't available to you on discovery."

He shook his head. "You're bluffing."

I smiled my best and most mysterious smile and stepped around him toward the stairs. A grinning Nero walked beside me. I said, over my shoulder, "See how you like the newspapers on your back for a while."

We went downstairs and out of the courthouse. I had a moment of bravado as the sun beat down on us.

"Come on," I said. "While the dice are hot we'll go down and beard the lion in his den."

"That's very original language," Nero said admiringly.

I ignored him.

Garran's mill was a ramshackle structure in the east end of town. There appeared to be people working around it, and it was large, but it didn't seem to me that enough money could come out of it to support that house I'd seen on the river.

One nervous, obviously harried typist sat in the outer office. Framed and mounted on the otherwise bare walls there were little homilies to remind her of her duties: *Eight Hours of Work Is Good for Body and Soul* and *A Penny Saved Is a Penny Earned* and *It's Better to Light a Candle Than Curse the Darkness*. I wondered how she could work with all those platitudes to read and study every day.

"I'd like to see Mr. Paul Garran," I said.

"Your names?"

"Sam April and Nero Crabtree."

"I'll see. You wait." She turned from us and went into a rear office and was gone for a while.

She beckoned to us when she came back out, and Nero and I went past her.

Paul Garran sat behind a kidney-shaped desk. Behind him, framed and mounted on the wall, were his various delegate badges from state conventions and pictures of a younger, slimmer Garran photographed with state and national politicians, famous and infamous.

It seemed to me that Garran had lost a bit of weight since last I'd seen him. There were dark circles around his eyes, but the eyes inside the circles were still cold and calculating. They calculated me now and found me wanting. He didn't bother to rise.

I sat down unbidden. I nodded at Nero and he sat down also. "Mr. Garran, this is Mr. Crabtree. He's assisting me in the defense of Alphonse Jones. You'll remember the case, I'm sure."

He nodded and waited.

"I'd like to ask you a few questions. If you don't care to answer them here, then you can answer them in court."

"Don't threaten me, young man. I've been around a lot better lawyers than you'll ever be. I'll listen to your questions and answer them or not answer them as I see fit."

"Would you please tell Mr. Crabtree and myself where you were last night between the hours of, say, eleven and one?"

He thought about it. "Put that one down as none of your business."

I smiled. "We feel it is. Your name keeps coming up as we investigate what really happened in the murder of Julia Cunnel and the killing, last night, of Mrs. Calling."

His voice became belligerent. "What do you mean my name keeps coming up?"

I watched him. Suddenly his face seemed set in stone. I owed him nothing, so I went on. "Your wife mentioned you were out of the house the night Julia Cunnel was killed. Julia worked for a lawyer who died without making a will, even though he was a probate specialist. Your wife inherited his money. You sold Al his house. You could have had a key to the shed lock. And Julia Cunnel's death might have benefited you, she being a possible witness to a will, if there was one, and to what Sanders, the lawyer, actually thought of you and yours. Last night Mrs. Calling, who knew something about what happened that night in the graveyard, got hoisted up and hung on a beam in her house." I watched him. "Do you want to tell me anything about any of this?"

"No," he said.

"Then I suspect we'll see you in court."

"Maybe. I'll watch the papers. I may need a long vacation soon. Let's see you subpoena me off a cruise ship, peanut brain."

I shook my head. "Leave if you want. Your testimony is important enough in this trial that I'll bet there'll be no completed trial without you. Evidence such as I related to you can and will be related by others. The only thing that'll happen if you go off someplace is that you won't be around to defend yourself—if you have any defense."

His voice was harsh. "I didn't kill Julia Cunnel."

I got up and Nero followed suit. "So you say," I said. "I'll get answers to what I want in the trial." We went on out of the office. He still sat there. I looked back at his face, but it was unchanged.

I wasn't completely disappointed with the interview.

It was clouding up when we came out of Garran's mill. On the way back to the office it began to rain.

12

I FIGURED A decent interval had passed and that I could see the Cunnels. I did it alone; Nero thought his presence on the scene might irritate them.

The Cunnel home was old but well kept. It was still raining when I got there—a cold rain, good for grass, bad for people.

They were polite enough. Mrs. Cunnel was almost gracious, but I could see pain lines around her eyes and her clothes hung slackly on her. I went into the house with them.

Mr. Cunnel said, "We don't hold with what a lot in this town have to say about you, Mr. April. Some people seem to think it's your fault you have to defend that animal, but Julia worked for a lawyer and we learned from her that even guilty people have a right to a fair trial. Besides, executing him won't bring Julia back, and my wife and I hope we're not vindictive people."

I sat back in a somewhat threadbare chair and sipped the hot coffee Mrs. Cunnel had brought me and watched the rain strike like little hammers against the windows. She sat opposite me, birdlike, her hands thin claws in the uncertain light of the gloomy day.

"I really thank you people for talking to me," I said, watching Mr. Cunnel. His face was hidden in the shadows of the wing of his chair. The room seemed empty and gloomy, as if I were at a private wake.

"Julia was an only child?" I asked.

"We had three, two boys and Julia," Mrs. Cunnel said

carefully. "One of the boys died very shortly after birth. Joe, the other boy, was killed in Vietnam. Julia was the only one left." She put her head down, but she didn't cry. All her tears were gone.

"Did Julia ever talk about any of the particulars of her work at Mr. Sanders's office?"

Mr. Cunnel answered. "She never said anything. At first we asked her questions, but it made her angry. She considered it a confidential position. She'd talk about general things, but not about anything that went on in the office."

I tried again. "Did she ever say anything to either of you about someone threatening her or Mr. Sanders because of any case they were in?"

My question seemed to puzzle them more than anything else. He shook his head. "All we knew was that she worked for Mr. Sanders and he paid her a certain amount of money every week. She wouldn't even talk about her work after Mr. Sanders was dead and she wasn't working for him anymore."

Mrs. Cunnel added, "One time she came home early from work and I asked her why. She said Mr. Sanders had been taken ill. I had to wait to see it in the newspaper to find out what was wrong with him, that he'd had a heart attack. She was closemouthed. I could tell her a secret of my own and know it would be the end of it." She smiled wryly. "She never told me any of hers." She rocked back in the chair, the thin smile fixed on her face. Her hands restlessly fidgeted with her dress.

"Was she going with anyone particular?"

Mrs. Cunnel nodded. "There were always men around." She looked at me and smiled a bit more warmly. "She was rather fond of you, Mr. April."

"Me?"

Mrs. Cunnel leaned forward. "She'd seen you at a few parties and she used to talk about you. She thought you looked nice. And you're in her diary. She kept one. I never touched it while she was alive, but I read it . . . after . . ." She stopped talking and turned her face away from me.

A diary. My mind reached out at half-formed ideas.

Mrs. Cunnel collected herself. "There wasn't much to it. Just a few scribbled lines about shows she'd seen and liked or whom she'd seen at a party. I think she even kept secrets from it. There wasn't anything about the office except the date she was hired."

"I wonder if you'd let me see it?"

I thought for a moment she was going to refuse, but Mr. Cunnel nodded to her. She got up painfully and went to the stairs and up them.

When she was out of earshot, Mr. Cunnel nodded. "She's not well. All this has been very hard on her." He leaned forward in his chair. His own face was cadaverous in the dim light. "I hope," he began, "I do hope that this will be over soon."

"I'll try to leave soon," I said, misconstruing his words.

He waved a hand. "That's not what I meant. I meant— oh—I don't know what I meant." He sat back in his chair again and fell silent.

There was a fireplace in the room and I found myself watching it, although there wasn't any fire there. The house and the people in it were like that fireplace. Once there'd been much warmth in the house, but then another war had come and the flames had flickered and some of them had died, but part of the fire had remained, burning carefully, with small dreams. Now all the fire was gone.

Mrs. Cunnel came back and handed me the diary. I went carefully through it while they watched me.

It was a five-year diary and it would have run out at the

end of this year. Julia must have started it in high school. At first it was copiously kept, but then it began to slack off and the entries became fewer and shorter. There were Cokes at the drugstore and an occasional movie that impressed her enough to take pen in hand. Once there'd been a trip to Atlanta to see a play. There was a lot about the play.

In the past six months the diary had begun to pick up again. There was a little about Ken Cavin, none of it very revealing. He was "cute." There were whole pages rhapsodizing about a trip to the capital and maybe renting an apartment there and a struggling painter named Michael. "My only dream man," the diary described him. He must be the one Ken Cavin had talked about. I was going to have to see him. If there was a key to Julia Cunnel, he might hold it. I wondered if the Chevy would hold up for a trip to the capital.

You could see a little of the girl in her diary. It was like her. Not a great deal to the girl; a fairly pretty girl, looking for something, not knowing exactly what it was and not really finding it. A girl who'd been married to her job and someday might be lucky or unlucky enough to marry some guy like Ken Cavin (or me) and begin to hate him as the years passed and dreams faded. Small sins, small pleasures.

My name was in the book twice, both times before the grand affair with Michael, but near the end of the diary. I'd made an impression. Once she'd seen me with Doc Mahoney at a party we'd gone to. She thought I looked mysterious. There were also a few squibs about dates with Doc. She thought he was "rough," whatever that meant.

There was nothing about the office, nothing about Garran. I closed the book carefully. "Thank you for letting me see it," I said. "I'm glad she liked me because

I liked her very much." That was a lie, but a nice one. "Can I ask you to let me borrow this book until the trial? That won't be long and I'll promise to take care of it."

Mrs. Cunnel nodded. "If you want," she said. She smiled and let the smile die away. "She'd been going up to the capital a lot right before she was killed. She said she'd met a nice man up there." She frowned a little. "We didn't like her going out of town by herself, but now I'm glad she did, that she enjoyed herself."

"How about phone calls?"

Mrs. Cunnel nodded. "A few. She had one right before she went to the movie that night. But she answered the phone herself and never said who'd called."

"When you answered the phone for her, did you ever recognize who it was who was calling?"

"No." She shook her head. "She'd run for the phone whenever it would ring. She was so secretive, so afraid we'd find out something about her. She'd never say to us who called and I learned not to ask."

I got up. "Please don't say anything about the diary unless the police or the prosecutor want to know." I nodded at them. "Thank you for your help. Thanks also for the good coffee."

Mrs. Cunnel said listlessly, "Won't you have some more?"

I shook my head. "No thank you." I shook hands formally with Mr. Cunnel, nodded to Mrs. Cunnel, and got out.

Outside the rain was still falling and it was still dingy, but it seemed almost cheerful after the house. I walked out to the car and looked back from it at the house. There was no light coming from the windows and no one to wave good-bye. Water poured down the rainspouts onto a lawn that needed cutting. A few flowers waved listlessly back at the rain, like minor-league hitters at big-league curves.

I drove back to my apartment, where Nero waited. I told him about the Cunnels and the diary. At the apartment we read the local paper. There were double headlines. The first was about Mrs. Amanda Calling's death, which the paper intimated was at the hands of a sneak thief. The other was about the motion to dismiss. The newspaper was up on Rhinehoff's back. There was even an editorial that questioned his competency. At no place in either story was there any indication of a possible link between the two murders. In the story on my motion to dismiss, I was punished obliquely for my frivolous delaying tactics.

Nero smiled at me when he'd read the stories. "Your local newspaper has no gamesmanship. Also no ability to report factual things that don't agree with what they want to happen."

I looked him over. "Yeah."

"How now?"

"Maybe we'd better go to the capital tomorrow?"

"Yes," he said. "We better had."

I found Michael Reardon in a studio apartment in a building that was proceeding quickly toward tenement stage. To find him wasn't as hard as I'd anticipated. I went to an art-supply store and checked on the Michaels who bought supplies. I asked about age and looks and they came up with a name to fill the bill as Julia's "dream man." Nero, in the meantime, was checking the records on Paul Garran.

I knocked on the door a couple of times and Julia's dream man came.

The sun shone through a window behind him, lighting his back and not his face. I could only make out one thing for certain. His right hand was one of those iron claws, such as they give out for what's commonly called valor or sacrifice.

"I'd like to talk to you about Julia Cunnel," I said.

He hesitated, but only for a moment. "Come in."

I followed him in. The apartment was crowded with canvases, all of them angry blobs of surrealistic color. They hung from the walls, they sat against the sparse furniture, they were stacked in corners. In the center of the room, where the best light was, there was an easel. I couldn't see the picture there.

He read my eyes. He held out the mechanical hand. "No great demand yet for a right-hander learning to use his left."

My chest ached and I reached up and touched it; he saw the movement and read it.

"Nam?" he asked.

I nodded.

He wasn't handsome, but maybe he had something better. He was tall and slender and his eyes and overly angular features had an eagle look, perhaps something like the questing, eager look that Julia Cunnel had owned. His movements were quick and sure, his clothes dirty and paint-stained, but his face seemed clean and so was the remaining hand.

He nodded. "I knew her." He smiled a little. "She picked me up one night. It was like she'd been looking for me. She came to see me a lot after that." He looked down at the floor. "Would you like to see her picture?"

I looked at the angry pieces of surrealism around me and he figured out what I was thinking. He laughed and went to his easel and I followed him.

The portrait was Julia Cunnel. He'd captured her perfectly on the stretched canvas, the eyes, the half smile.

He spoke so softly that I had to strain to hear. "I thought I'd lost it when I lost the hand. All I could do was paint colors and crap like you see here, but I've got it again." He smiled.

I turned and looked out the window. In the distance, this clear day, I could see the stockyards. On an unclear day I figured I could at least smell them if the wind was right. The dirty city lay outside his window and it brought back to me memories of another city, far north of here, of law school and what once had been but no longer was. I looked back at the picture.

"She was in love with you," I said. "I know that much."

His voice was sorry about it. "I know. I couldn't help it. I tried to stop it a few times."

I believed him.

He wasn't watching me. He was explaining it to himself. "She was going to come here to live. I told her that no one could live with me. She said she knew a place to get some money, enough for us to go to Mexico and live together." He looked up at me and moved his good hand restlessly to cover the other. "I told her I'd go." He shook his head. "It was a chance. She knew I was ashamed to take money from her, that I didn't love her and can't love anyone now or ever maybe, but it was enough for her. It was what she wanted."

"How much money?"

"She said maybe fifty thousand dollars."

I nodded. "So she went back home. She had someone there she thought she could extort money from. She tried that and the person killed her."

"I guessed that when I read the newspapers."

"Where were you the night she was killed?"

He hesitated again. Finally he said, "I was down there. She was supposed to meet someone at quarter to twelve. My bus got in about eleven. I waited for her at a tavern called the Oasis. She never said who she was going to meet. She was supposed to come, but she never did. I took the last bus back at one o'clock. I read about her in the papers next day."

I looked again at the picture. I didn't think this man could have painted her picture in the way this one was painted and still have killed her. But I could be wrong. I'd been before.

"I'm going to have to subpoena you," I said.

He nodded agreeably. "I'll come testify if you need me."

I examined him again. I thought that he might never have been in love with Julia Cunnel but was in love with the picture of her he'd painted.

I gave him my card and went back out into the sultriness of the day.

I was supposed to meet Nero back at his office. It was downtown. I walked to a main street and after a while got a cabbie who was either dumb enough or unafraid enough to cruise the area.

Nero's offices in the UIM building looked pretty plush. I went in one of those doors that opened when you got close to it. There was a honey-colored girl behind a modern desk. She looked up at me inquiringly.

"Yes?"

"Sam April. Has Mr. Crabtree gotten back yet?"

She nodded. "He's been expecting you." She smiled at me. "His office is the first one on the right."

His door was open and Nero had his feet propped up on his desk. He was reading a detective magazine, one of those kind that report the "facts." He twitched the cover and a poisoner on the cover sneered at me.

"Don't let me disturb you if you're right in the middle of a juicy murder," I said.

He smiled and got up. "News can wait. Come on, I want you to meet someone."

He took me down a long hall to another office. Inside, a frail old man sat behind a desk that was piled with letters and folders.

"This is my boss, Mr. Wilson. This is Sam April."

The man behind the desk didn't get up and I could see why. His chair was a wheelchair. He reached out his hand and I took it and his grip was strong, but cold.

"George Washington Wilson," he said in an unexpectedly heavy voice. "My people once had the unfortunate habit of giving their children the names of American heroes. I grew up in those times." He looked at Nero. "Quit calling me your boss. You never do anything I tell you."

Nero smiled and folded himself into a chair. I did likewise.

Wilson's eyes inspected me. "I'd expected to see someone seven feet tall, from the way Nero talked. Well, how's your Jones's case coming?"

"Better," I said.

Nero looked at me. "Tell all."

I filled him in. I told Nero about Michael the painter, Julia Cunnel, and the money.

Nero nodded. "Good stuff. I got some, too." He handed me a card. "Exhibit one: an arrest-card copy on Paul Garran. Assault and battery. The charge was filed in 1969 and later dropped. Here's something else. I had to pull some strings to get this. It's a commitment record out at Suncrest. Expensive and very private. He was in there for more than a year."

He handed me the other papers. I looked at them. *Dynamite*. They were the tools that might dig Paul Garran's grave.

"I couldn't find out a lot about the arrest, but the cop who made it is still on the force. I've got his home address if you want to see him."

Wilson nodded at us. "Well, get at it. Don't waste time on me."

Nero got up and so did I. We were at the door when

Wilson said, "Good to meet you, Sam. Come again." Nero smiled at me out of the side of his mouth and we went on out.

We walked down the hall. "Tough man," Nero said. "They had to take both his legs off. He's got diabetes and can't last much longer. He's also got a photographic memory. I've seen him, in trial, recite back testimony word for word, from days before."

"He did trial work, then?"

"Did it? He does it now. He'll be doing it up to the day they dig a hole for him."

We went out past the honey secretary and Nero winked at her. "I'll come back for you sometime."

She smiled, seemingly not unhappy about the prospect.

"Where do we go to talk to this cop?" I asked.

"I've got his address," Nero said.

We walked a block down the street in the busy downtown part of the city to a parking lot and got Nero's Plymouth, which we'd driven instead of the Chevy. Nero muscled it through traffic until we reached a residential area. He parked in front of an inexpensive house. Nero pointed at it. "Cop's name is Williams. I'll stay or go. The boys at the station I talked with said he's kind of a redneck."

"You think I'd get more alone?"

"Maybe."

I got out, went up a lumpy walk, and knocked on the door. A big man in an undershirt opened it and looked belligerently out at me.

"We don't want any."

"I'm not selling anything. I'm a lawyer and if your name is Williams, I'd like to talk to you."

"Williams is the name," he admitted. He reached his right hand down and scratched idly at his bay window. "Talk ahead."

"I'm checking on a man named Paul Garran. Arrest records show you picked him up about fifteen years ago for an assault and battery. Can you tell me anything on it?"

"Nah. Too long ago."

I persisted. "This probably didn't turn out to be an ordinary case." I smiled at him and shook my head. "All right. We'll subpoena you then. Maybe you'll remember more in court when I lay his arrest record in front of you."

His eyes didn't change. He wasn't afraid of me or my subpoena, but having to testify made him think again.

I started to turn away.

"Wait a minute," he said. "Come inside."

I followed him into a dim front room filled with wicker furniture. From a window an air conditioner made rumbling noises. A black and white television brayed a beer commercial and he tuned it down. We sat down across from each other in the wicker chairs and the seat of mine probed me.

"I remember a little of it, but it's a long time. This guy, Garran, beat up some old bastard in a bar. It was while I was still a riding cop and we took the call. Later an assistant in the prosecutor's office asked me to forget it. Said the guy went nuts and his wife was committing him."

"How about the man who got beat up?"

"Some bum. The bar was tough city and what some guy like Garran was doing there in the first place was beyond me. At least that's what I figured out the way it washed out. He must have had money and spent money to fix a charge like that."

"Who was the assistant prosecutor?"

He thought a minute. "I think it was Ellison." He laughed a barking laugh. "He won't do you any good. He died a couple of years back. Heart attack."

"How bad did Garran beat up this guy?"

He looked up at me. "Bad. He used a knife. The bum almost died." He looked down at the floor. "This was a tougher town then. They told me to let it alone, so I let it alone."

"Who told you?"

"The assistant, but he'd be talking for someone up the ladder."

I talked with him a little more, but there was nothing else, and I thought I was getting almost all of the truth, except for how much he'd been paid to forget it. He escorted me to the door—a big, tough cop, running a little to fat now, perhaps sorry for some of the money that had bought the flab.

The outside seemed overbright after the dimness of Williams's front room. I walked up the street to where Nero was parked.

"Anything?" Nero asked when the car was in motion.

"Some more," I said. I told him what Williams had told me.

"Used a knife, eh? That's better and better. It's after three. Let's go someplace and get us a drink. I'm going to have to stay over. They've been having some employment problems out at a new housing project they're building and the old man's going to need me for a while. You can take the bus back later."

"Sure you don't need to go back to the office?"

Nero looked me over placidly. "I don't want to spoil them, Samuel. I just want to keep them reasonably angry at me."

13

We went to a place Nero knew. It had a long bar and was already crowded in the early afternoon. The bar was black. There were some tables in the back and we sat there. A couple of large, dark men at the bar looked me over with some hostility when we came in, and after a while a waiter checked with Nero on me. Nero said something to him in a low voice and ordered two beers.

"Let 'em try to water that," Nero said, when the waiter had gone.

I looked him over. "I think I'm going to subtly push this thing at trial, Nero. I'll trade Rhinehoff an early trial date for a nonjury trial."

He nodded. "I was talking to Mr. Wilson. He knows Weeks and says he's OK, and that's my feeling also. If you can get it done in front of him without jury, we might have a chance. Subpoena all your witnesses before the news breaks."

"How soon should I try to set it?"

"As quick as you can. Give me a week or so here and I'll be ready to help. Try to set it in two or three weeks. Rhinehoff will be willing to trade anything for an early setting."

"I doubt we can break Garran."

He shook his head. "That's not the point. You couldn't break him any better six months from now. Al has to be found guilty beyond a reasonable doubt. So we give Weeks what we've got. We ask for a separation of witnesses. We run in everyone else and let Garran sit in the hall and watch. Under a separation, if we watch it and have the judge admonish the witnesses, he won't know everything we've got. Call him last and hit him hard. Reasonable doubt's all you need."

"I'd give my fee for that will."

He shook his head. "You'll never find it. He's probably burned it. His story is that Sanders tore it up. That's enough without any evidence to the contrary. Surely he's long ago destroyed it. Has to have."

We drank the beer and then another. We went to another place and then another. Most of them were black places. A curious thing has happened to places that cater to blacks. They don't like white customers. Maybe it's from the long history of the black race in America. We used to keep them out from public places and in some ways still do. But I was with Nero that night. Most of the places knew him and that made me all right.

We tied a pretty good one on.

I remember bits and pieces of it. I remember one place where tall black girls danced without clothes and another where the smell of marijuana almost drowned out the smell of alcohol.

We switched to Scotch. Candy is dandy, but liquor is quicker.

At one place I remembered Nero staring at me. "They're going to get him," he said.

"Who?"

"Al," he said. "We're going to work our butts off and put up the good fight. Maybe Weeks won't give him the death penalty because we've done such a good job, but he'll get a term of years that will mean he'll die in prison."

"I don't think it'll be that way," I said, not sure at all.

Nero looked me over with cynical eyes. "Do you think being innocent or guilty makes a difference in this state where you're talking about the rape and murder of a white woman by a black man? Ask the old man in the wheelchair sometime. Ask him how many he's defended where there was only a crappy case but the defendant got stiffed? No, Sam boy, Al is wrapped and packaged. Judge Weeks wants to be judge again. He's not up next time, but he's a politician. He'll take care of his own. You'll see."

I shook my head stubbornly. "I got a feeling also. We're missing something. Maybe it's something I saw or something someone said to me. I know it's there. A thing that'll break this case wide open if I can find it and use it."

His eyes regarded me with minor interest. "I hope you remember it." He smiled. "Tell Al to keep his chin up when you see him. I'll be down before the trial, but probably not until right up on the time for it."

I looked at my watch. The hands swam before me. "If you're not going to take me back, then I ought to get to the bus station."

Nero nodded. "I'll take you outside and get you a cab. I don't drink and drive in this town."

I said, "I used to in my town, but I don't anymore."

I got the last bus and went back. I was pretty intoxicated, but I could still think. And all the way back I thought and thought, but nothing came of it. There was just Nero and me on one side of the chessboard. On the other side of the board there were all sorts of someones. One of them had Garran's face, but he wore a sheriff's badge and drove a red Mustang convertible with a painting of the Mona Lisa on the side. His doctor's bag lay beside him/them.

I fell asleep. I dreamed my dream again, a dream for these times. The bombs were falling, sun-hot around me. There was a figure who kept throwing a switch. He had a black mask for a head. I ran until my chest hurt and my own head fell off at the top. I awoke when the bus rolled into my town and it was better. I went home and slept some more. My dreams there were about being in a place where it was hot and dry and my chest didn't hurt. Craftily, I didn't tell anyone I was a lawyer.

In the morning I went to see Al at the jail. I told him we were going to set the case for trial at the earliest possible time.

He asked, "Is that big guy you brought in here going to help you try it?"

I nodded.

"And he wants it set for trial?"

"Yes."

"Then let's try it."

"OK. One thing, Al. If anyone asks you about the early trial date, I want you to bitch about it, raise hell, say we're dumping you. I don't want the word to spread in here and get back to the prosecutor that you want a quick trial. If it does we lose some bargaining power. No one gives something for what both sides want."

He considered me. He was not without guile and intelligence. He nodded.

I left the jail and walked to the prosecutor's office. On the street I saw people I knew. Some spoke to me; some didn't.

Rhinehoff was alone in his office. He beckoned me in.

"The grand jury will consider the Jones thing again tomorrow morning," he said gruffly. "Here's a list of the jury."

I looked them over. "They seem OK," I said. "I'm sure there's no one I'd want to strike." I handed it back. "I don't think we'll want to bring Al over."

His face got a little red, but he didn't say anything.

"Paper's been on you pretty hard," I said. "You must not be number-one man on Garran's list now."

"I'm a little higher than you," he said. He nodded. "That's not very high. He wants it tried bad."

"You got your discovery stuff ready?"

He handed me a medium-size file. "If you want, I'll have my girl shoot a copy of Jones's complete file and promise nothing else will come in. In writing."

"What else would you trade for a quick trial date?"

"A lot," he said.

"I've got some stuff. I want to get it in without a lot of trouble. If I'd go for an early trial date, would you go easy on the objections?"

He thought about it warily. "My case is circumstantial and open and shut. It's a cinch. I put mine on and then you can do about anything you want to other than smuggle the defendant another ax."

"And we try it in front of Weeks alone? No jury."

He shrugged. "Weeks has convicted people before and sentenced them to death. Bench trial is agreeable with me. It'll save time."

"Then how about two weeks from Wednesday?"

He nodded. Desire turned to suspicion. "Why, Sam?"

I shrugged.

"You've got something, haven't you? Why not just give it to me? If you can show me the man's not guilty, I'll give the evidence to the grand jury. I'm dead with Garran anyway."

"I don't have that kind of evidence. I swear I don't. I've got a boyfriend of the girl who was in town that night, but I'm only calling him to show he was in town and what their plans were. I'm going to call Garran and his wife because of their work situation with Al and because they owned his house. I'm going to present some stuff on Mrs. Calling. All I've got is maybe some possible doubt."

He nodded.

"I want one more thing in return for an early setting. I want you to hold off announcement of trial date for a couple of days after we agree and Judge Weeks approves, so that I can subpoena my witnesses before any of them run."

"You're going to subpoena Garran?" he asked, relishing it.

"And his wife."

"Jesus, Sam. He don't like me, because I didn't do things just right for him. He'll track you for twenty years if you embarrass him."

"I've got some stuff to embarrass him with."

He shook his head. "I don't want to know about it. I want to be able to say I didn't know about it and I want your promise to back me up."

"Happy to oblige."

"Go hard," he said.

"Also, I've got the dead girl's diary in my possession. I want to introduce it."

"What's it say?"

"Nothing. I'll let you look at it in the privacy of my office if you say nothing about what's in it and don't question it when I have it marked in."

He shrugged.

"I'll do one more thing for you in return for giving me a free hand. I'll tell the newspapers, if anything works out, that you helped me set it up to serve the ends of justice."

"Do you still believe in that blind bitch?" he asked.

"Only now and then."

I could see my offer appealed to him. He couldn't lose. If Al was convicted—and I knew he was sure he would be—he got credit for bringing it to a quick trial and getting his man. If I pulled off the impossible and Al was freed because I showed he wasn't guilty, he still got the credit.

He nodded. "You got it, Sam." He held out a hand. "Friends again?"

I shook it. We never had been, but now perhaps we were.

We called Judge Weeks and confirmed the trial date. I went to the clerk's office, got blank subpoenas, and took them back to my office and made them out. I subpoenaed everyone in sight: Garran and wife, Jefferson Jones, Doc Mahoney (although I knew the state would call him), Ken Cavin, Michael Reardon. I left out Tarman. He'd be around anyway.

I looked over Rhinehoff's file. There was nothing there I didn't expect.

I waited.

A couple of weeks isn't a long time. My subpoenas were dutifully served and the news of the impending trial broke in the newspaper. Every once in a while some caustic ass would call me on my phone and raise hell.

My business, during those days, dropped off to almost nothing in most respects, but it had never been much anyway. It did pick up significantly in one way. A lot of black people came into my office over the waiting time. I wrote wills for elderly people with little to will. I wrote deeds and contracts where none had before been considered necessary. I settled property-line disputes and gave advice. And I got paid for most of it. So I lived. I checked and rechecked and read advance sheets and dusty law books on the law of murder, whole transcripts from other cases. Some of it rubbed off and helped. At least it made me a slightly better lawyer.

Mostly I worried.

Jan and I went out the night before the trial began. I was tense and on edge and took up my usual occupation—drinking too much. Otto's was uncrowded and dim and the beer was cold. We held hands across the table. The jukebox played Michael Jackson in the background and I liked it, even though I usually couldn't stand Michael Jackson.

"How's my lawyer?" Jan asked.

I sipped beer. "I'm fine."

"You've lost some weight." She examined me critically. "You've got brand-new crow's-feet at the corners of your eyes."

"I'm getting up there in years."

She initialed her glass with hers and mine. "What are you going to do about us, Sam?"

"What do you want to do?"

She smiled. "I want to have half a dozen kids, all of them underweight, all the boys with crow's-feet at the corners of their eyes."

"That's nice, but not now."

Her face lost expression. "Sometimes I think I've gone wrong getting involved with you. I keep wondering if it'll always be this way. The next case. No time for us because you're too deep in a new someone's problems. I know you're the marrying kind, Sam, because you've got a readable track record. What I don't know is whether you're the kind I ought to marry. I need and want too much. I don't think I could stand it if we got married and the marriage became like lots of marriages these days—you going your way, me mine, all dry and dusty, obligatory sex on alternate Saturdays." Her eyes were wise and wistful. "There'll be other cases like Al's and they'll breed more of the same."

"One at a time," I said. "Death cases aren't that frequent. There may be other cases up the line where I feel strongly, but not like this one. I think Al's almost surely innocent and yet he stands a good chance of dying. I think he has a chance of getting off if I'm clever enough and mean enough." I looked in her eyes and tried to make her understand. "You called me tolerant once. I hope I am. I wasn't born that way. I got my degree under fire. When I got these holes across my chest that you stroke so gently, it was a black hospital corpsman who dragged me back and started blood soon enough to keep me from dying. So I owe for that. I can't repay it, but I can try. I think it's wrong to believe that a man's guiltier because he's black than he would be if he was white. A jury here would feel that way."

"Is that why you avoided a jury trial?"

"Sure."

"Some of the people in the office have speculated about why Rhinehoff let you do that."

"Let them ask Rhinehoff. Nero and I think Weeks will be as fair and honest as he can under the circumstances."

She nodded. "Thanks for the short course in Sam's law." She ran her hand through the smooth blond hair in a gesture as old as time, yet new and exciting as I watched. After a while we got away from the serious.

14

NERO CAME DOWN the morning the trial began. We went together to the courtroom and I had Deputy Jenston bring Al over.

It was a nice day outside the courtroom, but it was desolate inside. Washington frowned down on us from his picture above the judge's bench. The sky might be blue outside the windows, but inside I turned on all the lights and the room was still cheerless.

I thought the strain was getting to Al, but he was handling it pretty well. He came into the courtroom with only a touch of shamble to his walk and he answered quickly when we asked him questions. But inside his eyes the fire seemed banked now. I believed he was seeing the final burning when the boss man threw the big switch. His eyes seemed to be waiting for us to help him step down the line toward that time.

The courtroom began to fill and by the time Rhinehoff arrived it was full to overflowing. If Rhinehoff was worried, he showed no indication of it. My own stomach went queasy at the sight of him. He was a veteran and I was a tyro at this sort of thing.

Nero leaned over. "Smile and look mysterious." He leaned back in his own chair, smiling and polishing his cuff links with a white handkerchief. I tried to follow his example, but I suspected my own smile was weak.

Rhinehoff made a predictable opening statement and Nero and I waived ours. Our own case was based mostly on what the police hadn't done, on how they'd looked no further than Al.

If our waiver of opening statement affected either Rhinehoff or Weeks, it wasn't apparent.

When Rhinehoff had completed, I did get to my feet and say, "We request a separation of witnesses, Your Honor."

He nodded, very businesslike. "Motion granted."

"I'd further like to request the court to instruct each witness that they aren't to discuss any questions asked with any other witness."

He was unsurprised. "That's a part of the separation process, but I'll warn each witness if you want me to." He nodded at Rhinehoff. "You tell yours. I don't want any mistrial here." He looked at all three of us. "Is the prosecution ready?"

'Yes, Your Honor," Rhinehoff said.

"Is defense ready?"

"We are, Your Honor," I croaked.

Weeks leaned back impassively, "Prosecution may call its first witness."

Rhinehoff said, "Prosecution will call Doctor Ambrose Mahoney."

"Ambrose?" I whispered to myself.

Nero grinned at me.

"Doctor Mahoney and whatever witness you designate may remain," Weeks said to Rhinehoff. "I assume you want the sheriff?"

Rhinehoff nodded. Ben Tarman came up and took the empty seat beside him.

"All other witnesses will leave the courtroom and hold themselves in readiness outside. I admonish the witnesses, singly and otherwise, they're not to discuss this matter while this trial continues."

I'd agreed with Nero that he'd handle most of the state's witnesses and I'd do the examination on those we'd subpoenaed. I thought this might work best because I knew many of the prosecution witnesses and might be easier on them than Nero.

I stared out at the packed spectator seats. Jan sat in the front row and she gave me a hopeful smile.

Mahoney took the stand and I looked him over. As usual he was carefully dressed and, also as usual, he looked tired and worn out. I hoped for his sake that none of his patients picked this day to give birth to a baby.

He was sworn in and told the court, in a matter-of-fact voice, his name, his medical experience, and the fact that he was county coroner.

"Now, Doctor Mahoney," Rhinehoff asked, "did you have occasion, in your capacity as coroner, to examine the body of a person known to you as Julia Cunnel on or about the seventh of June of this year?"

"I did."

"How and why did this come about?"

Mahoney was brusque. "Someone had struck her several times on the head with a sharp instrument. She died almost as soon as the first blow was struck, within minutes of it anyway. There were signs she'd then been raped."

"What sort of signs?"

"She was bruised, her clothes were disarrayed and torn, and her lower undergarments had been removed. There appeared to be some internal bruising also, but it was less evident, having happened very near the time of death."

Rhinehoff picked up the ax from his counsel table and had it marked.

"Did you run a blood test on the blood you obtained from this ax and match it with the blood of Julia Cunnel?"

"I did. They matched."

Rhinehoff moved on. He led Mahoney through every

gory detail, first in medical terms, then translated into lay language, perhaps for the spectators in the courtroom.

I watched Judge Weeks. He had a pad in front of him and he drew diagrams on it and wrote things from time to time. His face was emotionless. Sometimes, when there's a jury, you can tell how testimony affects the jurors by watching them. At first they're curious and they covertly watch the defendant for his reactions as the evidence is received. Then, when things begin to pile up, they quit watching him, because an inner decision has been reached. It can be countermanded, but it's difficult to do. An instructor in law school once told me that the more vicious and senseless a crime is, the easier it is to secure a conviction before a jury. Jurors feel instinctively that a vicious crime must be punished. Because there's an indictment against the defendant, he becomes the logical choice. But watching Judge Weeks told me little. His eyes flicked here and there and he made his notes and that was it. He betrayed nothing of what he thought.

I also watched Nero while the testimony droned on. Rhinehoff established, through Mahoney, where the body had been found and that the crime had been committed in our county and state—venue—without which the case wouldn't have been provable. Nero entered no objections. His face never changed.

He made his first objection when pictures of the deceased were offered into evidence—and was, of course, overruled. Julia Cunnel lay as they'd discovered her, skirt up high, thighs spread. Her eyes were open to the night sky, but they saw nothing. Behind her head, in the dust, there was a halo of blood.

Eventually it got to be noon.

We recessed and Deputy John Bob Jenston herded Al back over to the jail for his lunch. Nero and I walked back to the office, picking up sandwiches on the way. There was a grinning, gaping crowd hanging around the courthouse. Some of them had been inside the courtroom, some not. They whispered and frowned as we went past.

We got Mahoney at a little before two, when Rhinehoff finally tired of wading through gore. We'd worried through the noon hour about what to ask him and then decided against asking anything at all.

"Your witness," Rhinehoff said.

Nero got to his feet. "We've no questions of this witness now, but we may wish to call him during our defense. We've subpoenaed him."

A little ripple ran through the courtroom when Nero sat down. Al reached over and touched my arm, and I could see the questions in his eyes.

I leaned close to him and whispered, "Don't worry about anything that happens during the state's case. Just listen."

He nodded and sat back.

The next witness for the state was Sheriff Ben Tarman. He was sworn in and gave his name.

"Do you hold an official position in this county?"

"I do."

"What position is that?"

Tarman leaned forward. He looked tough and competent. His hair was combed and, for once, he was wearing his dentures. His big gun was steady against his hip.

"I'm sheriff of this county," he said.

Rhinehoff smiled. "Did you have occasion, Sheriff Tarman, to visit the home of one Alphonse Jones on the night of the seventh of June or, more correctly, early in the morning of June eighth of this year?"

"Yes, sir."

"For what reason did you go to the defendant's home?"

"I was assisting the local police in the investigation of the killing of Julia Cunnel. We investigated several nearby houses. Inside the nearest one to the scene of the crime we found the defendant Alphonse Jones. He was asleep or pretending to be asleep in his bed, but the lights were on in his home."

"Did you have a search warrant?"

"We did. We called you and had you make one out, and I went with you to the city judge. You swore me and asked some questions, and then the city judge, he signed the warrant. I went back to the scene and had one of my deputies and a city policeman check the shed while we searched Jones's house. They had to pry open the shed. I got called back there and we found the bloody ax. We then arrested Mr. Jones and brought him back to jail."

Rhinehoff held up a hand to stop Tarman. He picked up the ax, which had been marked State's Exhibit A.

"I hand this to you. Is this what you saw in the Alphonse Jones shed that night?"

Tarman leaned forward. What he was looking at really wasn't an ax or a hatchet, but an implement about halfway in between both. Its handle was too long to classify it as a hatchet and too short for an ax. It looked like an ax blade someone had attached to a homemade handle.

"It is," Tarman said.

"You're positive?"

"Yes, sir. There's a nick in the blade. The one I saw in the shed had a nick in the same place." He smiled. "Besides, I've had custody of that thing since the night Julia Cunnel was killed and kept it under lock and key in my property room. I have the only key to that room and I was the one who put it in there and got it out this morning."

Rhinehoff nodded. "All right," he said. "Now, you said the shed was locked?"

"Objection, Your Honor," Nero said, rising. "Witness testified that entry into the shed was made by one of his deputies and a city police officer."

"Sustained," Weeks said without looking up.

Rhinehoff nodded. "After you talked to the defendant and read him his Miranda rights, did the defendant ever tell you the shed had been locked that night?"

"Objection again," Nero said.

Weeks smiled. "If this were a jury trial, Mr. Crabtree, I'd probably sustain your objection because I've not yet heard the Miranda warning that was given, but I'll hope that such was given and will certainly not take into account anything the defendant said if the Miranda was insufficient or defective." He nodded. "Now, can we get on with it?"

Nero sat down.

Rhinehoff took Weeks's hint. "Do you have a card you read to persons who may be accused of crime, Sheriff?"

"Yes."

"Did you read it to Alphonse Jones that night?"

"I did."

"Do you have that card on your person now?"

"In my billfold." He got it out.

"Read it," Rhinehoff said.

Tarman read the standard Miranda warning.

"After you read Mr. Jones that warning, did you then ask him about the shed?"

"Yes. He said it was locked and he had the key. I asked for it, but he wouldn't tell me where it was. He said it was his key, not mine."

"Did he say the ax was his?"

"He said there was a short-handled ax in the shed that belonged to him. When we showed him the bloody one, he said nothing."

"Did you find any other ax in the shed?"

"No, sir."

"And did you have occasion to examine the shed itself after the ax was found?"

"Yes. I examined it some that night and more the next day. You could tell where my deputy and the city officer helping him had pried the hasp off. I also looked over the lock. No one had forced it open."

"Then anyone entering the shed, in your opinion and based on what you saw, would have had to have a key?"

"Objection," Nero said. "Calls for a conclusion."

Weeks nodded. "It may be the sort of conclusion the witness can make. If not, I'm certain you'll show that to me on cross, Mr. Crabtree. Objection overruled."

"Yes, sir," Tarman said to Rhinehoff. "Well, there was a little window on the north side of the shed that was open, but no one over five years old could have gotten through it."

"How big was the opening?"

"Maybe one foot square."

"Did you ask the defendant any other questions on the night of the murder?"

"Not after he said he wanted a lawyer. But when we went to his door and showed him the search warrant, he said he'd been drinking."

Rhinehoff looked over at me, then turned back to the witness. "Did Alphonse Jones say or do anything else when you went to his home?"

"Well, we had a few words. He's like a wild animal sometimes. I've had trouble with him before when he was picked up for—"

Nero was on his feet. "Objection. Will the court please tell this witness to answer only the question put to him?"

Judge Weeks nodded. He leaned down to Tarman and said, not unkindly, "You'll answer only the question asked."

"All right, Judge," Tarman said tranquilly.

Rhinehoff proceeded. He had Tarman point out the

defendant and asked that the record and transcript show the identification. He had Tarman describe the condition of Al's house at the time he and his deputies and the city police had entered. After a while he turned Tarman over to Nero.

"Sheriff Tarman," Nero said, "how long have you been sheriff of this county?"

"This time three years. Before that I was a deputy. I was sheriff for eight years before that. All told I've been in the department almost twenty years."

"And during this time have you ever had an occasion to investigate a murder when you didn't have a confession in hand?"

"Well, we've had our share of local killings, I guess, but no real murder cases before this one," Tarman answered cautiously. "This is a small town."

"Then you've never investigated a real murder case before?"

"I suppose not, if you exclude those other things."

"But you investigated this one?"

"I sure did."

"And you were the man in charge of the investigation of this case?"

Tarman hesitated and I could see what Nero was driving at. I could also sense that Tarman was reluctant to say he wasn't in charge.

"I guess I was as much in charge as anyone. I had the state boys to come in and help us on fingerprint stuff and looking for clues, and the local police were involved, too. We all helped crack this one."

"I'll then ask you if you helped in the investigation of another killing, at Mrs. Calling's house a few weeks back?"

"Objection," Rhinehoff said. "The death of Mrs. Calling is irrelevant to this case."

Nero looked up at Weeks and smiled. "I think we'll be able to show relevance as we proceed, Your Honor."

"What is it you intend to prove?" Judge Weeks asked mildly.

"That the two murders could have been committed by the same person or persons and that the defendant, having been in jail on the night of the Calling murder, couldn't have committed it."

Judge Weeks nodded. "I'll let it in."

Rhinehoff was still up. "Your Honor, I want to continue my objection. The experts who've looked at these cases don't see any connection between the two murders."

Nero nodded. "We've just found out how expert your experts are, Mr. Rhinehoff. I'd rather have the court make a determination of whether there's a connection or not than your so-called experts."

"Continue your cross-examination, Mr. Crabtree," Judge Weeks said.

"I've forgotten the exact question," Tarman said.

"Read it back to him," Judge Weeks ordered the court stenographer.

"Yes, I investigated that murder also," Tarman said.

"And once again you didn't have a killer in view, someone who'd admitted to murdering Mrs. Calling? Second time in . . . what did you say? Twenty years?"

"That's true, but the crimes were entirely different."

"Tell the court where Mrs. Calling lived, both in relation to the scene of the crime we're trying here and to the Alphonse Jones residence."

"Well, it was right next door to where the defendant lived and maybe two hundred and twenty-five yards from where the Cunnel girl was axed."

"Thank you," Nero said. He turned his back to Tarman and gave me a tiny nod. Then he turned back. "As to the case we're trying here, Sheriff, I'd like to know whether you did any further investigation in the neighborhood after you finished your foray through the Jones house."

Tarman leaned earnestly forward. "We talked to lots of people about what they'd seen or heard the night Julia Cunnel was killed."

"All with the intention of attempting to obtain more evidence against Mr. Jones?"

"No. We asked about him, but basically we asked what folks had seen and heard."

"And what did you discover?"

"Nothing."

"Did you talk to Mrs. Calling, the second victim?"

"Yes."

"What exact questions did you ask Mrs. Calling and the other neighbors of the defendant when you called on them?"

"We asked if they'd seen Alphonse Jones or anyone around the neighborhood at the approximate time the murder happened. Everyone claimed they had been asleep except Mrs. Calling. She said she'd gone inside." He nodded. "No one would admit to even seeing Julia Cunnel."

"Other than talking to a few neighbors, you then did no investigation at all? You felt you'd captured the murderer in Mr. Jones here and had enough evidence to convict him, and all your investigation after the fact was based on your conclusion that he was the killer of Julia Cunnel?"

"No. It wasn't that way," Tarman said, face reddening. "I was there when the state boys compared the fingerprints on some tape on the ax handle with Al's fingerprints. They blew them up and flashed them on a big screen and there was an expert there. He showed us they were Al's prints." He nodded reasonably. "If we'd have found other fingerprints, we might have looked further. If we'd have found anything, we might have done more. All we found was Al."

Nero watched him. "Sheriff, did you ever hear of gloves?"

"Objection," Rhinehoff said.

"Overruled," Weeks said. "This officer's on cross."

Nero asked it again. "Did you think about gloves?"

"No. It was hot out that night."

Nero asked, "Was there blood on the ax?"

"There was a lot of it."

"Were there any fingerprints in the blood?"

"No."

"When you went to the defendant's house, was there any blood on him or on his clothes?"

"Not that I saw. I didn't look too close. Maybe someone else did."

Nero smiled. "You were in charge. Did you check to see or have anyone else check to see if there was any blood on Alphonse Jones or his clothes or anywhere except the head of an ax you found in his shed?"

"He could have washed it off before we got there. We didn't find none, but the state boys said that didn't mean nothing."

Nero hesitated. I knew his thoughts. He could get the last part of the sheriff's answer stricken.

Judge Weeks looked down at Nero. "Don't spoon-feed me, Mr. Crabtree. I also know what's available to me and what's not." He smiled, unoffended.

"He just didn't get any blood on him," Tarman volunteered.

"Was there a lot of blood around the head of the murdered girl?"

"You saw the pictures," Tarman answered irritably.

"But in your expert opinion and that of your state men, a killer wouldn't have gotten any of it on him or his clothes if he'd killed Julia Cunnel and then raped her after she was dead or while she was dying?"

"It's possible."

"How about probable?" Nero asked.

"I'd say probable too. He was careful not to get her blood on him."

"But not careful about killing her within a few hundred yards of his home," Nero ended for him.

Tarman shrugged. "If you want my opinion, I think he was drinking and he saw her and had to have her. . . ."

Nero's voice was as icy as I'd ever heard it. "You just answer the questions, Sheriff. If I want you to theorize I'll tell you." Nero turned to Judge Weeks. "I'll ask the court to strike the last remark."

"It may go out," Weeks said laconically.

Tarman's face got red again.

Nero looked back at Tarman. "I'll ask once more. The defendant wasn't careful about killing Julia Cunnel near his home, was he?"

"No."

"But you say he was careful about not getting her blood on his clothes or on himself?"

Rhinehoff got up. "Your Honor, counsel is trying to harass the witness."

Weeks smiled. "I know of nothing in the law that keeps him from doing that, Mr. Rhinehoff." He nodded at Tarman. "You may answer."

"Yes, the defendant was careful about not getting blood on himself," Tarman admitted grudgingly.

15

AND SO THE afternoon went. Nero continued to whack on Tarman until we adjourned a little after four. The main points of the story weren't shaken. The case was still strong on the ax, its inaccessibility to others, the proximity of the defendant to the scene of the crime, and his fingerprints on the smooth part of the ax handle and a taped area.

I stopped Tarman in the hall. He was a little cool, perhaps blaming me for the severity of his cross-examination.

"Did all the people we subpoenaed show up?"

He hesitated. "I'm not sure, Sam. Some of them were around earlier, but I guess they left when we told them it'd take a couple of days to put on the state's witnesses. We told them to return tomorrow."

"Check for me in the morning, Ben. See if they're all here. If any aren't, send me in a note."

He nodded.

I went down the steps with Doc and Nero. I was dead tired but figured I'd be up late. I turned to Doc outside. "Come up when you finish office hours tonight. I need to talk to you."

His strange eyes examined me. "To the office?"

"Yeah," I said. "I'll feed you some of my Beam. I've drunk enough of your alcohol in the last month or so."

"OK," he assented.

Nero and I had a bite and then went to the office. I was tired and Nero was worse off than I was. Trials are tense things. You sit in your chair waiting, trying to be perpetually alert. You stalk witnesses. You spend your moments trying to think what to ask. You feel it at day's end.

"How come you didn't pursue the Calling thing more?" I asked Nero.

Nero riffled through a law book. "I wanted to see first off if we were going to be able to get it in. I got out of Tarman what we wanted, that it isn't a part of a double-murder package." He shook his head. "Hey, Weeks is okay. I didn't think we had a chance, but maybe we do."

"If we can get anything out of Paul Garran," I said.

Nero looked at me. "Or maybe someone else."

Doc came about nine o'clock, just as we were about ready to give him up.

He squatted bonily in one of the hard-backed chairs I'd brought in from the hall. "I need to go home and go to bed," he said. "And if Mrs. Smith or Mrs. Brown calls me with labor pains, I'm going to tell her I've joined a labor union."

I opened the big drawer of my desk and got out the bottle of Beam. I poured three and handed one to Doc. He lifted it and smelled it, and I watched him and started mine toward my mouth. Doc, the connoisseur.

Doc came up fast from his chair, his red-rimmed eyes gleaming. His hand slashed across my face. My glass broke on the floor. I looked down at it stupidly.

Doc's voice was authoritative. "Don't put that to your lips, Nero. Bourbon's not supposed to smell like bitter almonds." He took the bottle from the desk, smelled it again, and then handed it to me. I sniffed gingerly. It did smell funny.

"I think someone's loaded your bottle, Sam," Doc said.

"Jesus," Nero said, looking down at his own untouched glass.

"Mrs. Calling's dogs died from cyanide," Doc said.

I looked up at the wall. My diploma hung there along with my admission certificates. I remembered other times I'd almost died, but this was different. The framed documents swam in front of my eyes.

This time was worse, much worse. I had Jan and I wanted to live again. I rubbed my hands together. They were oily and sweaty and cold all at the same time. Nero and Doc watched me.

"You didn't drink any, did you, Sam?" Doc asked.

I shook my head, unable to speak.

"You keep this office locked all the time when you're not here?"

"Most times," I said. "Sometimes I forget."

Doc shook his head. His face had regained color. "I told you a long time back what might happen if you started fiddling." He smiled nervously. "I hope you left Jan to me in your will."

"I promise to add a codicil in the morning."

Nero looked at both of us as if we were crazy. "Should I call Tarman?"

Doc nodded. "Not you. You picked on him all day. Me."

We'd calmed down appreciably by the time Tarman and Jenston came to the office and poked around for a while. They found nothing, but then we didn't expect them to find anything.

Tarman smelled the bottle. "You sure it's poisoned, Doc?"

"If you want to try it out, Ben, be my guest," Doc said.

"I'll take your word." He turned to me. "Got any ideas who did it, Sam?"

"A few," I said.

"Been a lot of hard talk around town on you," Tarman said.

I shook my head. "I know you, Ben, and I know

you're not that dumb. I think you know why this was done."

He nodded, not sure, but leaning my way. "Maybe."

"Then I want help—we want help."

He hesitated only momentarily. "I guess I'd help you if I could." It was a large concession and all of us knew it.

"All right. What I want is for you to keep an eye on Paul Garran. I want him here and available. You served him with a subpoena."

Tarman shook his head. "I got to remembering after you asked me. All your witnesses showed up this morning except one. Mrs. Garran was there, but Paul wasn't."

I looked at Nero and he looked at me. "See if you can find him, Ben."

We parted.

I went home and tried for sleep, but it was an elusive thing.

Tarman was in his office early in the morning when I got to the courthouse. A crowd was already beginning to gather in the hall, waiting for the trial to begin again.

Ben shook his head. "I drove out there last night after I left you. Paul Garran wasn't home. Mrs. Garran looked like she'd been crying. She said he left the day after the subpoena was served. He said he'd be back in a couple of days but hasn't come back or called. She said she was going to call me about it but was ashamed to." He looked up at his ceiling. "I still don't believe it."

I kept my face impassive. "He's run, Ben."

"What for?" he asked. "Why?"

"You'll hear it soon enough in court. We had some incriminating evidence on him. I think he had a good idea it was coming."

When Nero came I told him. He nodded.

"I hate to say it, but we're not hurt," he said. "I was talking with Rhinehoff outside. He's got enough witnesses to last until maybe the middle of the afternoon.

Most of it's blood-test and fingerprint stuff, plus the local officers who were at Al's house."

"You handle them," I said. "Tarman and I are going to go hunting for Garran."

"He's long gone."

"Probably. I want a look."

He surveyed me thoughtfully. "I can handle it, but you'd better check out with Judge Weeks."

When Weeks came I requested a meeting and explained that one of our witnesses had failed to appear after being subpoenaed, that Sheriff Tarman and I were going to look for him, and that I'd be back before noon.

"I'll give you a continuance until then if you'd like," he offered courteously.

I shook my head. "No need. Mr. Crabtree will be handling the witnesses this morning. And we'll waive, on the record, any necessity for me to be here."

"How about your client?"

"I'm sure he'll waive my being with him also. If not, then we'd like to have that continuance."

"So be it," he said.

I got Tarman and we took his Pontiac and drove out to the Garran house. Tarman had already called Mrs. Garran and told her not to come in until we came out. She was waiting for us at her door.

Her eyes were puffy, but the house was antiseptically clean. She led us to a bedroom.

"After Sheriff Ben brought the papers out, Paul became very agitated and said he was going to leave town for a few days." She looked over at his bed. It was neatly made, but a few rumpled clothes still lay on it. They looked as if they'd fit Garran. "He packed a little bag and left." She looked at me. "He took his gun."

Tarman asked, "What gun?"

She fought to control tears. "He's kept one around here for a lot of years. I looked and saw it was gone after he left."

"Did he say why he was leaving?"

She shook her head and seemed unable to answer. "He took the old Ford," she finally sobbed.

I nodded. Tarman patted her hand.

"Have you any idea where he might go?"

"No. He seldom went anywhere without me. Except to town and to his clubs."

"Will you come to court this afternoon and tell the judge about his leaving?"

"I suppose it's my duty to do that."

"It could save an innocent man's life."

She nodded. "I'll be there."

We went back outside into the heat. It was now the tag end of summer and the trees were beginning to get a few yellow leaves. I walked to the side of the house and looked down at the big, muddy river below me. I tried to reason. Garran's flight, after being subpoenaed, should about clinch it. But somehow it didn't seem exactly right and I was unsure.

Tarman came and stood beside me. "You know when I decided to help you, Sam?"

I shook my head.

"When that black lawyer with you didn't ask me about my relationship with Julia Cunnel. You didn't tell him about that, did you?"

"No. It wasn't germane. You didn't kill Julia Cunnel. I thought maybe Garran did, but now . . ."

I looked back at the house. Mrs. Garran watched us forlornly from out her big picture window.

"When we get to town," I said to Tarman, "would you please drop me at the First National Bank?"

"Sure."

I looked Al over when they delivered him from jail that afternoon. I watched him and I couldn't smile. Not yet.

"I think you'll be a free man before dark," I said.

His eyes came up and met mine and he could see I meant it. His shoulders straightened. Something came into his eyes that had been missing when I'd first talked to him at the jail. He reached out and shook my hand. "I believe you," he said.

Rhinehoff had finished just before noon, instead of his estimated two o'clock. It was our turn now.

"Your Honor, the defense will call Mrs. Thomas Cunnel," I said.

They called her in the hall. "Only a few questions, Mrs. Cunnel." I got the diary and had it marked.

"Can you identify this?"

She looked it over. Her eyes were still somber pools and she'd lost more weight. "It's my daughter's diary."

"And your daughter's name?"

"Julia Cunnel."

I looked at Judge Weeks and Rhinehoff. "I move it into evidence." I handed it to Rhinehoff. His jaw tightened.

"No objection, Your Honor."

I nodded at Mrs. Cunnel. "No more questions."

Rhinehoff looked up, startled. "No questions," he said.

I called Tarman over. "Lead her out past the other witnesses and make certain no one talks with her."

He nodded.

"Then bring in Mrs. Garran."

She came in and her eyes looked worse than they had that morning. She took the stand and was sworn in.

"State your name, please," I asked, kindly.

"Minerva Garran."

"You're the wife of one Paul Garran?"

"Yes."

"Were you present when your husband received a subpoena to appear in this trial?"

"I was."

"Tell the judge about his reaction."

She nodded. "He became agitated. He said he was going out of town for a while. He went quickly and packed a bag and took off in one of our cars, an older-model Ford."

"Did he say where he was going?"

"No. He said he'd be back in a few days, but that's been a long time now."

"Have you heard anything from him?"

"No. I've called places where I thought he might be, but I haven't found him yet."

I looked up at Judge Weeks, who was watching Mrs. Garran with interest.

"Your Honor, that's all we have to ask of this witness for now, but we'd like to reserve the right to recall her when Mr. Rhinehoff is done."

"I've no questions," Rhinehoff said. "And no objection."

Mrs. Garran went back to the hall. I called Michael Reardon. The formalities were observed; I got his name, occupation, and a little of his background into the record.

"On the night of June seventh of this year, were you with Julia Cunnel?"

"Yes." He wasn't looking at me. He was observing his claw hand.

"Tell the judge what happened."

He nodded. "She was supposed to meet someone that night. That person was going to give her fifty thousand dollars. All I had to do was wait and then help her spend it. I waited in a bar for her, but she never came."

"What bar was that?"

"The Oasis."

"Did she tell you who she was supposed to meet?"

I saw Rhinehoff getting antsy, but then he looked up at me, smiled, and nodded his head.

"No," Reardon said. "She said she'd meet me about

twelve. Then we'd leave for Mexico and I could paint there."

"That's all the questions I have," I said.

Rhinehoff looked at me and then at Reardon. "Do you mean she was blackmailing someone?"

"I don't know."

Rhinehoff looked inquiringly at me, but I shook my head, not knowing anything more.

He shrugged. "No more questions."

Reardon got up gratefully from the witness chair.

"Wait in the hall," I ordered. "We may recall you."

He nodded.

"Call Doctor Mahoney," I said.

Doc came in and took the witness stand.

"You're the same Doctor Ambrose Mahoney who testified earlier?"

"I am."

"And you realize you're still under oath?"

"Of course."

"I'd like an opinion. Can rape be simulated or faked? In other words, could someone have made it seem the Cunnel girl was raped when actually she wasn't?"

"I guess it could be done," he said, thinking about it. "It'd be kind of silly, but anything can happen.

I looked up at Judge Weeks. "Your Honor, could I have about five minutes of your time and Mr. Rhinehoff's time in chambers?"

Judge Weeks looked mildly surprised. Rhinehoff stood up, welcoming what I'd requested. "We'll go along with that, Your Honor."

16

I asked them to clear the courtroom for the last act. It wasn't essential it be done, but it seemed better.

Judge Weeks shook his head. "I can't do that, Mr. April. I'd have to hold a hearing, find reasons, and make a special order."

"I don't want it completely cleared. News media can remain. They'd be the ones to complain. If they don't complain and the defendant and the state agree, it can be done."

"Why do you want it done?"

"Because there's been a lot of heat on this case. I want this last part of it heard without any heat at all. I want a chance at this witness without there being a hostile group of spectators in there watching, grinning along the walls, and whispering among themselves."

Rhinehoff agreed. Weeks grudgingly agreed. We went in and made the record on it and the sheriff cleared the courtroom except for media people.

I called the last witness I wanted—Minerva Garran.

She came in and stared around the almost empty courtroom and I could see she didn't like it. I had her reidentify herself.

"How long have you and Mr. Garran been married?"

She looked up at the judge and over at the prosecutor, trying to read something from them. "More than twenty-five years."

"What did you do before you and Mr. Garran were married?"

"I was a nurse."

"You told me once, Mrs. Garran, that on the night Julia Cunnel was killed you were home, but your husband was out of the house. Is that correct?"

"Yes."

"You also told me your husband took care of all the business in your family?"

She nodded. "Yes, he did that."

"Don't you keep an account at the local bank, Mrs. Garran? Over at the First?"

"Oh yes. For little things."

I nodded at her. "I see. Your husband doesn't have an account there. He doesn't have a safe-deposit box, or a checking or savings account except the business account for the mill. How many safe-deposit boxes do you have in your name at the First?"

"Five," she said. "For jewelry and papers. Things like that."

"And do you have both checking and savings accounts?"

"Yes. I don't like to talk about them is all."

"How much do you have in those checking and savings accounts?"

"I don't know for certain. A substantial sum."

"And are there also stocks and bonds in your safe-deposit boxes?"

"Some."

"Are those boxes and accounts all in your name, or are any of them in joint name with your husband?"

"They're in my name. Paul wanted it that way because of being in business and politics. He thought someone might sue him." Her eyes had grown hard. "And most of the money was mine. It came out of my family."

"The Sanders estate?" I asked.

"Yes," she admitted, her face sullen now.

"About that estate—didn't you ever think it unusual

that your uncle, a lawyer, had died without leaving a will after cutting you out of the last one he executed?"

"He undoubtedly intended to make a new one."

"But he destroyed the old one before doing that?"

"Whatever he had, he must have destroyed. None was ever found."

I could see calculation on her face. She started to say more, then checked herself.

"Did *he* destroy it? Or was it your husband? Mrs. Garran, don't you secretly believe that your husband killed your uncle and destroyed the will that left nothing to you?"

A couple of the media people looked up, interested. Jan wasn't among today's crowd. Someone else was covering the trial today for the local paper.

The calculation hardened. "I don't think I should say. I don't believe you can make me testify against my husband."

A newsman watched her, punched his next-seat neighbor in the ribs, and began to scribble.

"You know, don't you, that your husband was committed once after he tried to kill a man in a barroom fight?"

A small but audible murmur came from the line of media people. The judge frowned, lifted his gavel and tapped it. Quiet came again.

She shook her head, now calculating me and what I knew.

I held up the records. "Here are records of both the commitment and the charge. I can get a police officer out of the capital down here to testify about them."

She was silent. Then she nodded, making her decision. She sat back in the chair and let her body relax, and she was, somehow, old at that moment. Her voice was so soft that I had to strain to hear her.

"All right, he killed him," she said. "Paul killed my

uncle and tore up the will because he refused to change it back. The mill was in trouble—bad trouble."

"And he then killed Julia Cunnel?"

"She asked him for money—a lot of money. He told me she knew about the will and was going to tell if he didn't give her money."

"And you were going to let an innocent man be convicted and go to the electric chair?"

"I was afraid to do or say anything. You don't know Paul. He's crazy—isn't that proof?" She pointed to the papers in my hand.

"And Mrs. Calling?"

"He was afraid she'd seen him go into the graveyard that night. So he killed her. He said it didn't matter about her. She was old and sick."

A newsman in the front row of seats craned to watch.

I had enough now. I could leave it where it was and no one would ever say I'd done wrong. Al was safe, out of the shadows. But I had to go on. I could feel beads of perspiration running down my back. The courtroom smelled of dust and mold. The faces around me were indistinct. All there was in the world was Mrs. Garran and me.

This was the time. If it didn't work now, I'd have lost, even with Al off.

I moved close to her. "Mrs. Garran," I said, "where is your husband Paul now?"

"Now? I don't know."

"Yes. You know. Tell it all."

She started to laugh, a hideous, crazed sound that rang through the mesmerized courtroom. "Where is he? Where? Why, he's in the river," she said, spacing it between shrieks of manic glee. "I put him in the river in his old Ford car." Her laughter subsided, and she went on more naturally. "You bothered him and harassed him and he was scared. I was afraid he'd try to blame things on me or hurt me once you got him here. I couldn't let that happen." She smiled, pleased with herself and her solution. "But he won't come here now, will he?"

She seemed to come to her senses. She took a handkerchief out of her bag and dabbed at her eyes.

I picked up the diary. "Mrs. Garran, I'd like to read you what it says in Julia Cunnel's diary for the night of June seventh." I opened the diary and thumbed through it as if seeking a passage. "Ah, here it is. It says, 'I'm going to meet Mrs. Garran tonight. Then I'll have the money.' Wasn't it you she was going to meet?" I held the book out as though to give it to her. As I hoped, she drew away from it and me as if we were vicious animals and would bite her.

"Filthy little sneak," she said softly.

"You knew how to make it appear as if she'd been raped because of your training as a nurse." I held the diary out again. "Please look at this and then tell the judge you weren't the one who killed Julia Cunnel."

Again she refused to touch it. Her eyes examined it, but she couldn't touch it. It was, I believed, a symbol to her of her own guilt. I was happy she didn't take it, since the page I'd supposedly read from was blank.

"I'm glad she's dead," she said.

"Of course," I said. "Tell me about it." I looked toward the back of the courtroom. People were intently listening back there. One reporter started to get up, but Weeks gave him a stern look and he sat back down.

"The little bitch was trying to blackmail me."

"You, not your husband?"

She looked at me and smiled bitterly, still not quite sane. "I told her I'd give her the money she wanted." She nodded to herself. "I made up my mind I'd not give anyone any of that money. It was mine. Paul kept extra keys to all the places he'd sold. I found the one to Alphonse Jones's shed in among them. It was simple. I knew what kind of lock it was because I went down there that afternoon to look the area over again. I drove past Mrs. Calling's and past his place. No one paid any attention because lots of cars go into the graveyard with flowers and the like in the daytime. Alphonse was in his backyard and I saw him put the ax in his shed and lock it. I opened the shed door that night and got the ax. I used it on her. Then I used my hands and did what I had to do to make it look like someone had been after her. I put the ax back in the shed." Her eyes watched me, suddenly venomous. "It would have worked except for you. I was around that neighborhood so much that I was part of it. No one ever saw me going or coming. No one ever said I'd been there that day."

"Did Mrs. Calling see you?"

She shook her head. "Maybe she heard me. I parked two blocks away, but that old witch would sit out on her porch at all hours, listening, watching. I saw your car parked close later. I went to her house to find out what she knew. I asked her to lock the door to her dog run and she laughed and did it. When I got inside she was writing a note to you. When I was done with her I had the poison. I thought the dogs might smell me out later so I put it in meat from her icebox and gave it to them." She smiled. "I didn't like them and so they died."

"I doubt Mrs. Calling knew anything at all," I said, twisting the knife. "Wait. Did you enter at the other end of the graveyard, away from Al's place, then drive through and park?"

"I may have. I guess I did."

"She could have heard your car."

She shook her head. "I wasn't certain, but I couldn't take a chance. I talked with you at my party and I believed I was safe. You suspected Paul. To make sure it stayed that way, I killed her. I used her extra clothesline. She was old and easy and she went quick. I hoisted her up. I hoped they'd think she killed herself because she was so sick. Then you had to be the one who found her." She shook her head. "Bad luck."

She inspected me with a sort of contempt, seeing me as some new sort of northern invader. The outthrust jaw had shrunk, but only a trifle.

"How did you kill Mr. Sanders?"

She smiled fondly, remembering. Her eyes sought approbation in mine. "That started it all and it was easy, too. He had a bad heart. I knew about pills I could get that would speed things up. He'd never pay for medicine if he could get it free. I went out to the house to see him after we got back on speaking terms. He was more mad at Paul than me anyway. So I gave him some pills. When he complained I gave him some more. He went running around his house like he was insane, all hopped up and high." She smiled again. "I think he figured I'd given him something bad. He went for his shotgun and I ran outside. He tried to shoot through the window and he turned on all his lights, but I got away into the dark and he died. It was really too late for him when he cut me out of his will. After he fell down I went back to the house and found the will copy he had there."

I made a mistake then. I looked over at Tarman and Rhinehoff. "Enough?" I asked.

Something in their faces warned me. She had a gun out when I turned back. She was bringing it up to center on me. I felt the way I had in dreams—nightmares. I couldn't move quickly enough. I lunged clumsily at her. Julia Cunnel's diary, which was lying on the corner of the bench, fell off into Minerva Garran's ample lap. She looked down and saw it there and then she screamed. The gun fell from her right hand and she brought the hand up to her mouth and sought a well bitten fingernail.

Tarman moved to her like an old bear and led her away. Her walk was shambling. I bent and picked up the gun, a small revolver, and handed it to Rhinehoff. I thought momentarily about the jail and wondered if the women's section was any better than the men's. If not, it was in for some heavy cleaning by a new inmate.

The courtroom was in an uproar. Newsmen clustered around me. I gestured for Rhinehoff to join me. We both smiled up at Judge Weeks.

"Here's the man who did it," I said, pointing at Rhinehoff. "He could smell it, too. He's more than a good prosecutor. He's a seeker of the truth."

Nero went out and released our other witnesses.

There was a lot of excitement, but after a while I went home. That night there were no bombs, no faces. There was blessed sleep.

I went back to the City Club two days after the trial ended.

I came in the door and they were waiting for me again. In a small town the people can be wrong. And if you're wrong with them, they'll accept that. If you're right and they're wrong, sometimes they'll accept that too.

"Here comes Sir Galahad," someone drinking at the bar said.

I started to sit at the end of the bar, but Doc Mahoney came and got me. He jerked his head and I followed him. His eyes were only mildly interested. "How long since you had a drink out of that office bottle?"

I thought about it. "A while. Since before Mrs. Calling was killed."

He smiled. "God helps fools. I checked your bottle. It was cyanide, all right. And did you notice she didn't confess to that? She's probably still hoping you get your nose into it."

The dentist and the real estate man were at our regular table. The only difference was that Sid Dart had pulled a chair up at the end. He looked me over and his face was expressionless. He had a large package on the table in front of him.

He said, "Open this."

I opened it. It was a cashmere sport coat. It felt soft and luxurious and looked as if it would fit.

"Try it on," he ordered. "Look at the label."

It did fit. I took it off and gravely examined the label: *Presented to Sam April from Sid Dart. This coat made of guaranteed 100% horse manure.*

Dart smiled. "I had to agree to pay these guys' lunch checks in order to sit here." He reached out a hand. "Can a pocket-edition pimp sit here, pay for lunch, and eat his words?"

I grinned and shook his tiny hand.

That night we had a party at Jefferson Jones's house. There was Al and Jeff and his wife. Nero came and brought the tall, honey secretary from his office. Doc came with a wild-looking nurse. Jan came with me. The house was old and tired and the floors squeaked when they were walked on. After a while we quit taking empty bottles to the kitchen and just stacked them here and there about the front room.

It was quite a party.

I drank too much. Four people had died and either Mrs. Garran would be in an insane asylum for the rest of her life or the state might exact another death before the matter was done. I didn't want any part of her situation. Thinking about Mrs. Garran made me feel like I was unclean. I didn't need to get drunk, but get drunk I did.

I remembered later standing against the wall. The windows kept blurring on me and the chairs had nasty lines to them. I was sure I wasn't supposed to sit in them. In the kitchen I could see gas flames burning with evil light as some party pooper kept calling for coffee.

And I talked.

"It was Paul Garran running more than anything else."

I moved my arm and slopped a little of my drink, but no one seemed to care. "He might have tried killing me, he might have done a thousand things, but I thought he was too tough to run. When she said he'd bugged out it didn't get to me for a time, but I guessed pretty quickly that she was lying. Someone *had* to be Julia Cunnel's killer. I'd thought it was at least possible that Ken Cavin or, less likely, Michael Reardon could have done her in. How could either of them, however, know of the ax and the shed? It had to go down quickly and silently. The killer couldn't even count on Al being passed out. That meant the killer had to have a key, be silent, and not get caught. Later that same killer had to know of and deal with Mrs. Calling's dogs." I pointed at Doc and grinned. "Now, Doc grew up on mad scientist and bug-eyed monster books and still reads them. He's like some lawyers I know who don't have a lot of use for people, but likes dogs or cats or horses. So I never considered Doc even when we met him near Mrs. Calling's house just before we found her. Her dogs loved him and he could do no wrong around them. With the doorway locked he'd not have killed them."

"See how easily I got out as a suspect?" Doc said to Nero.

"How about Sanders?" Nero asked, ignoring Doc.

I looked over at him. His massive form blocked part of the light.

"Hello, big man. When did you arrive?"

"You're out of it," he said. "I've been here."

"Never drunk," I said stoutly. "Just never sober."

"Sanders," Nero prompted.

"Yeah, Sanders. Rhinehoff called today. She's been talking ever since the sheriff put her in jail. She told Rhinehoff it would cleanse her soul. She said she gave him some ergo something-or-other or some pepto something-or-other. She ran and hid outside until he was dead after he'd tried to shotgun her. When she went back in she searched and found the copy of the will that was in his desk. Next day she ordered the office closed. She told Julia Cunnel the office was closed out of respect for Sanders. She found the other will and made a bonfire of the two of them. That set her up to inherit under the intestacy statutes. She said she'd waited too long for the money to give it up. She was frantic when Paul and Sanders had trouble. She made Paul make public truce with him. Then she killed Sanders."

I walked to the center of the room, but my feet weren't hitting at the right angle and I was slopping my drink again. "She and Garran hadn't slept together for years and she was still interested, so he wasn't that much of a loss." I looked around. Jefferson Jones was watching me, fear in his eyes. I check-reined my tongue. "All she lived for was the house and money. When she got them, she made sure she kept them. She found Mrs. Calling writing a letter to me. We'll never know what that letter was about. Maybe nothing at all. My guess is she was writing me about gardens or dogs or something innocent and unconnected. But it was enough to set Minerva Garran off and she killed again. That same night she got into my office and loaded my desk bottle." I looked around the room once more, focusing on them. "She was tighter than a well digger's butt in February. She had three cars out there. When she killed her husband, she carefully loaded him in the oldest one for his final trip. She probably begrudged him that." I slopped my drink again. "Whoops," I said.

I felt Jan take me by the arm. "Come on," she said. "We'll take a ride around and come back." She looked at me and I fell into her eyes, just as always. "We'll be back in a little while," Jan said to the rest of the party.

She led me out and got me into the passenger seat of the Chevy. The air cleared my head a little. I reached over and touched her face. She got the car in gear and drove for a time until we got to a pull-off space on the river road. I looked down from there and saw my little town of seventeen thousand shining beside the river and I felt better.

We talked for a long while. I began to sober up. We discussed serious things. We talked about her and me and us. And we did a few other things. But I was too drunk for much of that. After a while we went back to the party.

Al met me at the front door and his eyes looked me over as if I was ten feet tall and had come to town especially to hire him for the circus. He'd been drinking also, but all the shadows were gone from his eyes. Suddenly, I still wanted to be a lawyer.

"We were getting worried about you two," he said.

I nodded solemnly and turned to Jan. "Meet my fiancée."

I heard Doc's voice in the background. "Oh you poor, miserable bastard. I didn't care when you suspected me of murder, but I do care now. Why marry and make one woman unhappy when you can stay single and give them all a few fleeting moments of joy?"

I remembered something from the trial. "Shut up, Ambrose," I said.

Jan held tight to my hand. She smiled at Doc and Al and Nero and the rest.

If you have enjoyed this book and would like to receive details of other Walker mystery titles, please write to:

    Mystery Editor
    Walker and Company
    720 Fifth Avenue
    New York, NY 10019